The Dryden Arms

(House of Despair, a Comedy)

By Johnny Allina

ISBN: 151946343X
ISBN-13: 978-1519463432

For Leah Allina, the love of my life—her wit and brilliance elevated this novel to new heights.

Hell is other people.
— Jean-Paul Sartre, "No Exit"

CAST OF CHARACTERS

Astrid..................................

Brenda................................

Cortez..................................

De Soto.................................

Don......................................

Duncan.................................

Eli..

Hat Guy...............................

Heavyset...............................

Herman................................

Jonas...................................

Judy.....................................

Larry....................................

LoKey....................................

Magician................................

Marie.....................................

Maybelline.............................

Mikey...................................

Monique.............................

Orc.....................................

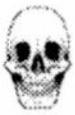

Rupert.................................

Vasco...................................

1

St. Patrick's Day, when the shots were fired, was the first time I questioned whether or not this had been a good idea.

I'd taken the position as Resident Manager of the Dryden Arms in Glendale, California, a suburb on the outskirts of Hollywood. It was a three-story, French Art Deco building put up by Douglas Fairbanks, Sr. in the '20s to house young contract players. I was supposed to be safe here.

Dealing with the tenants was a necessary evil. I, however, was a steadfast professional—unflappable. But on this night, my inherent nature was tested.

The situation between two warring tenants had clearly blown up that night. Jonas was your run-of-the-mill, loud, self-involved Hollywood hustler. Aspiring toward the gay Hollywood elite, he was on track as a "D-boy," or development assistant, meaning he read scripts for studio execs and scheduled their lunch appointments. Getting a reservation at Trois Mec was as crucial to him as solving the Iranian nuclear threat. Eli had the misfortune of living below him.

Making matters worse, Jonas was a die-hard, door-slamming, foot-stomping, loud-music-playing, cell-phone-yammering narcissist. He was notorious for singing along to his favorite Nicki Minaj songs. Loudly.

I'd inherited the role of mediator. Eli called me

often. And I paid many visits to Jonas. He feigned politeness as I did my best to explain the concept of apartment living. Jonas always promised to adjust his behavior. He didn't.

Eli, on the other hand, was just a regular guy. Quiet, stayed to himself, a loner, polite. Other than his calls to me about Jonas, I had no opinion of him whatsoever.

But I did feel bad for him on St. Patrick's Day. Jonas was extra-loud that night, maybe pre-gaming for a party, and all Eli wanted to do was relax after a hard day at work.

I told Eli when he called that I'd take care of it.

The music was blasting through Jonas's door when I knocked. I could feel the bass under my feet. I had to knock louder and louder until Jonas heard me.

He flung the door open. "Yo, Rupert. Come on in."

I think he was a little drunk or high, twerking. His boyfriend, Magellan, was splayed out on the beanbag chair, smoking a big, fat doobie.

"Want a hit, Rupe?" Magellan yelled so I could hear him over the music.

I politely waved him off.

"Jonas ... I need to talk to you."

"I'm not talking to you right now. I'm on a conference call." He tapped an earbud.

Since I wasn't in the mood to wait for Jonas to finish his call, I took out the notepad from my back pocket and wrote that he had to tone it down. Eli was getting stressed.

I held the note up in front of Jonas's face. He gave me a thumbs up.

Back in my apartment, sober and alone, I went to bed. Since I didn't have two black-haired Irish beauties to squire around getting shitfaced on this holiday night, I did the best I could. I closed my eyes and there they were, the two beauties, fully naked in a barn, teaching me to milk a cow. They were just squirting me with the udders when I heard two loud bangs. Was someone at my door, or were those gunshots?

The phone rang. "Eli's trying to kill me!"

"What?!"

"He shot at me!"

"With a gun?"

"Yes! Through the door."

"Really? So, where is he now?"

"How the hell should I know? He could be getting ready to come after you."

NOW I was worried. I made a move to crouch down in the bathtub, the safest, most insular nook in my apartment. It was as close to a panic room as I had.

Realizing that I could be in imminent jeopardy here, and I guess Jonas too, I knew I had to call for help.

"I'm gonna call the cops. I gotta hang up."

".... Yeah, hey Rupe ..." I punched off and dialed 911.

Ignoring all the texts that flooded into my phone from panicked tenants, two important thoughts occurred to me; first: I'd better give them the code for the security door, 'cause there was no way I was gonna go let the cops in and risk a possible lethal encounter with Eli en route; second: as I gave a physical description of Eli (Caucasian, male, five-eight, short brown hair, thin and wiry, glasses), I realized I'd just described myself.

I pondered a disguise, not wanting to be

mistaken for the shooter. Putting my contacts in would help. Throwing on my Dodgers baseball cap would conceal my short brown hair. But that would probably make me look even more like a shooter. I'd better just keep hiding in the bathtub, until the cops showed up.

Within a few minutes, red, blue and yellow lights were bouncing around as they reflected off the Art Deco tilework. Based on the number of screeching vehicles I heard coming to a stop, it sounded like they'd sent the entire Glendale Police Department. Good.

I was in no mood to call and offer comfort and crisis details to each and every tenant. I'd take the easy way out and send a mass group text informing them to stay in their apartments until further notice. That would get me off the hook.

Before I knew it, there was a powerful knocking at my door. I froze. Either Eli had come to get me, or I was saved.

"Glendale Police Department. Open the door!" It was my preferred option.

Nonetheless, I still opened the door with a great amount of caution. Keeping the chain on, in case it was Eli doing his best Glendale Police Officer impression, I saw a lot of shiny black boots and badges. I breathed a sigh of relief.

There were six of them, one more physically diminutive than the rest, but smacking of authority in stance and demeanor. He must have been the Captain. The other five, looking like ex-SEALs, guns drawn, were poised and ready, awaiting further orders from their leader.

"You the manager?"

"Yes, sir." God I wished I could have joined the military or law enforcement. But the whole getting up early thing wasn't going to work for me. And public, group showering was against my belief system. And I always had trouble with authority figures. But not today. I was pleased to be under the Captain's command.

"Where was the shooting?"

"306. Jonas's." I subtly cocked my eyebrows in that direction.

"And where's the shooter?"

Like I knew? "206. But he could be anywhere by now."

"We'll find him. You, stay!"

I assumed the wise Captain would leave one of the ex-SEALs stationed by my door, for my protection. They all left.

I wasn't about to go back in my apartment. For all I knew, Eli had shimmied across a series of window ledges from his apartment to mine and was sitting on my sofa, legs crossed, gun smoking, waiting to air his grievances about my failures to manage the Jonas situation. I'd stay in the common areas.

"Did you smell those cops?" Marie snorted as she beelined toward me. Her bony, off-angled frame housed an infinite supply of outrage.

Marie was convinced that her allergies to fragrances and scents could be life-threatening. But I Googled her symptoms and realized it was all in her head. She was a classic osmophobe, displaying fear, aversion or psychological hypersensitivity to smells or odors, which in her case branched out into bromidrophobia: a fear of body smells.

It likely stemmed from her years as a Glendale Unified middle-school teacher. Well, those kids did stink.

"You'd think civil servants would have been trained to know better. There are people with severely low fragrance tolerance. It's a complete lack of consideration."

"Good point."

"You know that plumber last week was ABSOLUTELY wearing scent. You have got to stay on those workers!"

"You got my text, right?"

"I didn't bother reading it."

"Well ... we did just have a shooting. There is an actual crisis going on."

"Eli finally blew his lid?"

"How'd you know it was Eli?"

"Come on. Who else?"

Judy emerged from the stairwell. In the fluorescent-lit hallway, her Kabuki-face powder, framed by jet-black dyed-hair gave her a vampirish quality.

"I was entertaining. What the hell's going on?"

What did Judy have to be annoyed about? This was mostly her fault, anyway. Jonas was her friend. She'd recommended him.

"How are my guests supposed to hear each other over this racket?"

"You know Jonas was shot at?"

"He's alive, right?"

"Think so."

"So how long before they wrap this up?"

I guess she wasn't too worried about her friend's near-death experience. "I really couldn't say."

As she turned to head back upstairs, a put-upon look on her face, I reminded both her and Marie that Eli was still on the loose. They seemed unconcerned.

I, on the other hand, was. Against Captain's

orders, I left my post and slowly edged down the hallway toward Eli's door. I needed to know what was going down.

As I rounded the corner, there was a buzz of activity. Based on my extensive knowledge from crime shows, I could tell they'd already gotten a warrant and were collecting DNA samples and doing a forensic investigation of Eli's apartment. Plus, I was tipped off by an attractive blonde's jacket with FORENSICS emblazoned on the back.

I bet if she let her tightly pulled-back blonde hair out of its ponytail, she'd look super-hot. I made my move, hoping she was single. "Hi, I'm Rupert. The building manager."

"Notice Judy's dress? Dolce."

Goddammit! It was Hat Guy, as the tenants had dubbed him, from 101. It made sense. He always wore vintage hats. Today, it was a black fedora. He was always smoking cigarettes too, and could just as easily have been called Nicotine Man or something of the sort. Now, he was blocking my move on the blonde with a totally irrelevant observation.

And what was wrong with these tenants, anyway? Could no one follow my instructions? I'd clearly sent an emergency text for them to stay inside their apartments.

"Ah ... I'm focused on the shooting."

"I knew it. I've been watching that guy. I've been afraid for me and Mikey."

It was Brenda—201, four-nine, stout, with frizzy red hair. I'd first laid eyes on her as she crammed a piece of mahogany furniture into her apartment. Not wanting to reveal myself, I'd watched her struggle with it. I would have offered to help, but I'd heard the tales of her poaching fine pieces from the elderly tenants on fixed incomes, once they died or moved out. They'd inherited these treasures when the building went from furnished to unfurnished. She was a predator. Her fluffy, white Persian cat Mikey, whom she cradled in her arms, was no better.

"We'll be rid of him after tonight." I told them.

Hat Guy cold-shouldered Brenda and sauntered off.

Brenda set Mikey down on the carpet, and he began doing crazy wind sprints. She cheered him on, tuning everyone else out.

"You're the manager, right?" I was interrupted again. Who was this dopey-looking, slovenly kid? Did he know what a nose groomer was, let alone a brush? "Detective Spooner."

This was a detective? This is what passes for acceptable? Were there no more standards? Where were the days of the sharp-suited, clean-cut, authoritative, respect-worthy law enforcement officer? This one looked like a refugee from an all-night kegger.

"I'll need to take your statement."

"But what's happening with Eli?"

The blonde chimed in. "He's been apprehended. They nabbed him pulling out of his garage. He claimed he was on his way to Ralphs to pick up some cake mix."

Wow. I didn't know Eli baked.

2

My immediate supervisor had asked that I confine myself to my cube and only communicate with coworkers electronically. Apparently, there'd been some complaints. This was at my former place of employment, a major international hotel chain's corporate office. And for legal reasons, I'm not at liberty to disclose the name. But it wasn't Marriott, Hyatt or Sheraton.

As their in-house copywriter, I was charged with making the concept of double points and double miles fresh and exciting every week. After week three, I'd run out of adjectives.

To stay inspired and mentally stimulated, some of my coworkers had to suffer.

Like that nasal-voiced, kiss-ass Korean girl who hugged upper-management types and would coo, "I missed you!" after a standard two-day weekend. She deserved for me to raise and lower her chair, ever so slightly, every other day, over the course of a year. When she gave her notice, I was the only one who knew why.

Or the ex-hockey player who was chronically at least four to seven minutes late to work and would blatantly cover his tracks by offering to fetch the department head a coffee and pastry of his choice. I'd find reasons to talk to him and was pointed and careful to drop key words out of our conversations, fueling his anxiety that he'd taken one too many hits to the head during his playing days and was losing his hearing.

It wasn't enough, none of it. In truth, what I'd wanted was for someone to just listen to me. Maybe these work antics were just an extension of my still frustrated childhood. If I dared open my mouth, I was shut down immediately. "You keep quiet." "You don't know what you're talking about." My mother and grandmother were two of a kind. Even my father didn't want to hear it. For my seventh birthday, I told him I wanted a fire engine. I got a blue, polyester Dickie, one of those mock-turtlenecks from the '70s.

There was the time my mother, grandmother and I were traveling back from a Florida vacation. When the ticket agent told us the flight had been oversold and we couldn't all board the plane, I tried to offer a calm solution. Eleven-year-old me offered to stay back and take the next flight. But they shouted me down. After much carrying on and not hearing a word I said, the two ladies boarded the flight and left me to travel later, on my own.

I would become a mime.

But it wasn't my calling. I was the worst one in all the mime classes I took throughout high school and college. And did no better at the adult mime extension classes. It was a coordination issue. I was regularly upstaged by a seven-year-old break-dancer in Washington Square Park and, oddly, drew fewer people than a hippie-type blowing gigantic bubbles through a plastic hoop.

The subways were fertile grounds for mimes. Usually, there was the guy with no legs on a furniture dolly wheeling himself with gloved hands through the cars, or mutes handing out printed cards and pencils for donations. Mimes would have been welcome, had aggressive mimes not spoiled it for the rest of us. First rule among New Yorkers: don't invade our personal space. The placing of hands in front of an imaginary wall didn't go over too well. Not when those hands went up in city dwellers' faces. I, along with my less aggressive brothers, caught the blowback—old ladies telling me to fuck off, children deliberately smearing my grease paint, umbrellas jabbing me in the chest ...

Writing, though, offered me a new way to be heard, to give myself a voice. But it needed a novel. Rich thoughtful fiction. Not "rich offers" for vacationers.

Besides, the copywriting made me a less-than-favorable employee. Frustration caused me to continuously and perhaps deviously act out at work.

So after numerous elevator rides to HR, when I was laid-off, I saw it as a gift. Not my supervisor. She too had been let go. Was I to blame? My offer of a coffee and pastry outing, as a form of closure between us, was rebuffed. Between sobs, I was blamed for her demise. Maybe she wasn't cut out to be a manager.

With unemployment and savings, I'd have three months to write and job hunt.

I ran down the money:

Groceries	$600.00
Gas	$29.67
Water & Power	$43.76
Cell Phone	$88.13
Cable/Internet	$135.66
Car Insurance	$92.37
Fuel	$120.00
COBRA (premium plan including dental & vision)	$426.04
Personal Entertainment (coffee & pastries)	$180.00
Mom's burial plot & perpetual care payment (negotiated with Rabbi Solomite)	$262.38
Publishers Clearing House subscriptions	$80.00
Rent	$900.00
Total Monthly Expenses	$2,958.01
Unemployment (w/o federal taxes taken out)	$1,800.00
Shortfall	$1,158.01
Savings	$3,660.00

To raise a novel from the dust, form it into clay and forge it in the kiln of my mind, I'd do a major life renovation.

At the time, I was living off the Sunset Strip. I had a cool single with sweeping views of the Hollywood Hills, Mike & Tito's Body Shop and the corner strip club that touted "All Nude" and "18 OK" in neon.

It was loud. Beer-bottle-breaking drunks stumbling out of the club at all hours kept me awake. It was almost a relief when the occasional low-rider crowd trespassed from East L.A., blasting Beyoncé and leaving 40s in its wake.

The tenants in that building were no better. Apartment doors slammed, would-be actors and actresses hung out on the front steps, spending their days sunning themselves and shouting minutiae back and forth—since apparently they had nothing more productive to do—and the wild tranny parties inevitably invited visits from the sheriff.

But worst of all, I was at the mercy of street parking. And between the strip club and body shop clientele, all the good spots got snagged, leaving the rest of us to troll the neighborhood, endlessly looking for a legal place to park. Once I secured a spot, I tried NEVER to move my car. I'd walk the 2.4 miles to work, unless it was pouring rain. And I lugged groceries up from Santa Monica Boulevard, keeping myself in stellar shape.

After a while, even walking in the neighborhood of gays and young hipster families became dicey. An unsavory looking guy, who I later learned had been lurking in the area, knocked a girl unconscious and was spotted by a neighbor stuffing her into the trunk of his Tercel. Thinking that seemed unusual, the neighbor yelled for help and rallied a passing gaggle of cross-dressers and transgenders. They were fierce and rushed the guy, who dumped the girl in the street and sped off. It gave me pause.

The high-stress living in Hollywood wasn't conducive to writing. I needed peace. I needed quiet. I needed to hear birds chirping, pigeons cooing, squirrels chattering. The rustling of leaves blowing in the wind. It was time to go.

3

I was on a mission to find the perfect place. I headed east, since west was too expensive. I found myself drawn to the foothills of Altadena, Pasadena and Glendale. The majestic old oaks that lined many of the streets and the smell of eucalyptus in the air told me I was on the right track. It was on day three that I rounded a corner in Glendale, and there it was.

The Dryden Arms announced itself in gold lettering on a handsome black awning. And it was grand. And there was a vacancy sign on the front lawn. Having a high credit rating, excellent references and winning good looks, I was a shoe-in. I jotted down the number on the sign and left a message.

I wasn't going to take any chances. I'd employ the Buddhist law of attraction and pick up some boxes outside Jon's supermarket and start packing, as if the place were already mine. I was a spiritual dabbler and Buddhism felt like the right horse to back. Their philosophies made sense to me, and they always served the best snacks and had the cutest women at their meetings.

Next day, Larry from the property management company called and said a unit was coming up for rent end of the month. We made a date.

When I got there and approached the building's entranceway, I spotted what I thought might have been a nautical theme. A lover of the sea myself, I could only hope.

It was almost too good to be true. The front door had a stained-glass window with a pirate ship design. I liked that the stained glass was hard to see through. It would afford me an extra degree of privacy. Yet I squinted through the panel and caught what I thought was a mini-pirate-ship-themed mosaic on the tiled lobby floor, as well as hand-painted scenes of sailing ships covering the walls. Perhaps, they'd gone too far.

"It's nice, yes?" Larry came up from behind.

A small man with intense blue eyes, he seemed like a nice guy.

Larry opened the door and led me through the lobby and up the two flights of stairs to 204, filling me in on the unique history of the building.

The apartment door had a coat of arms with three sails painted on it. The theme continued. Inside, the apartment was being renovated. An open ladder was propped up in the living room, paint supplies on a tarp and assorted tools lying around. It was huge, with high ceilings, crown moldings, a hallway leading from the front door to a beautiful, old Deco bathroom—a built-in vanity table with an overhead mirror between them—a bedroom that could house a family of migrant workers, a kitchen with more cabinets than I could ever fill and a dining nook you could seal off from the living room by sliding out a pocket door.

"You like it?"

"I love it!"

"That's good then."

"Can I ask how much?"

"For you, very reasonable."

"What's reasonable?"

"Let me ask you a question. How are you with people?"

"I'm a people person." It's what I assumed Larry wanted to hear.

"Then perhaps you'd be interested in my proposition. I'm looking for a new Resident Manager."

"What does that entail?"

"First of all, free rent ..."

I did a quick mental calculation.

Total Monthly Expenses	$2,958.01
Less Rent Saved	$900.00
New Monthly Expenses w/o rent	$2,058.01
Unemployment	$1,800.00
Shortfall with rent taken out	$258.01
Savings	$3,660.00

Less rent at the Dryden Arms, I'd have a year to solely devote to writing.

"I'm in!"

"And of course, managing the needs of the tenants on a day-to-day basis."

I had to think.

"It comes with a garage."

"I can do that." Living rent-free, parking included, was a lifestyle I could embrace.

"That's fine, Rupert. I can see that you're the sort to keep things running VERY smoothly."

Did I detect a faint accent? Under closer scrutiny Larry had the look of an ex-SS officer who'd skipped out on the Nuremberg trials and made his way to sunny SoCal. Property management was an ideal cover. What did I care, as long as my slightly Semitic nose didn't get in the way of free rent and parking?

We shook on it.

It was the end of a chapter, and the beginning of a new one in my young life. And in this new and improved part of my life, there'd be nothing IKEA. So I bequeathed my mismatched Swedish furnishings to my current, soon-to-be-former building manager, Jerry. I felt I owed it to him. Apparently, the feng shui totem that I'd been advised to hang over my door, and which brought me all sorts of good fortune, was wreaking havoc on Jerry. The off angle at which it reflected onto his door must have been the problem. Since I'd hung it, Jerry's pet rat Bob got cancer, his boyfriend dumped him and his car was stolen, although it was ultimately returned eleven days later smelling of egg salad.

In any event, Jerry was a good sport and helped me load the boxes into the U-Haul on the day I left Hollywood. I hoped Bob would make it.

DATE	TRANSACTION DESCRIPTION	PAYMENT, FEE, WITHDRAWAL (-)	✓	DEPOSIT, CREDIT (+)	$
11.29.14	Packing tape	14.73			3,645.27
11.30.14	U-Haul rental	126.47			3,518.80

4

My first full day at the Dryden Arms, Larry handed me a vendor list, a prison guard–sized key chain and a bottle of all-purpose cleaner, telling me to use it at my discretion. That was the extent of my training.

I was cleaning the metal faces of the lobby mailboxes—with a discretionary amount of cleaner—when I had my first manager–tenant encounter.

Of an indeterminate age—sixty, seventy, eighty, two hundred?—the woman had dead shark eyes and wore a standard off-the-rack workaday skirt/blouse combo. She stood with one leg at a rigid angle that made me think it might be wooden, without articulation abilities.

"You've got to make him stop."

"What?"

"Walking. He constantly walks back and forth."

I was puzzled.

"The old man in 302. It's your job to stop him." She indicated the spray bottle. "Is that toxic?"

I checked. "Nope." And underlined the word non-toxic with a finger.

"Make sure. I have severe allergies."

"Will do."

"And?"

Now the Walker couldn't exactly levitate. And

since he was two floors up, through a vacant unit, I marveled at the spindly creature's hearing, even despite the poor insulation. The building's owner, Duncan Danforth, kept 202 vacant for guests, a mistress, a mentally ill relative?

I wasn't sure how to broach the subject that most standard lease agreements did cover lessees' rights to perambulate within their domicile. I broke the news to her, gently. "He is allowed to walk in his own apartment."

"Not back and forth over the same spots! They're DEAD spots in the floorboards! This whole building's a noise-trap!" She went global. "Why do I have to listen to every phone conversation, the sound of recycling lids being dropped ...?" It went on.

I contemplated getting her some silent retreat center brochures. In the interim, I mentioned that I wouldn't be able to control every aspect of tenants' behavior.

She had a crazed look in her eye. "I need resolution. Tell him not to step on the DEAD spots."

Was the Walker supposed to play hopscotch in his apartment? I felt it was in my best interest to placate her.

"Let me see what I can do."

"I just told you. Rein him in!"

It occurred to me that I was dealing with a committed Solipsist. Someone with an extreme preoccupation with and indulgence of their own feelings and desires, coupled with an egoistic self-absorption. Should this tenant's feelings—or lack thereof—trump the other tenants' needs? But being a Solipsist, she had no understanding of the actual existence of others.

She gave me one last push. "Fix it."

I was now an acknowledged being in her presence, only because I was charged to do her bidding.

Upstairs, I knocked on the Walker's door. Waited. I didn't sense any movement behind the door. I knocked again. Louder. Nothing. I headed back to the seat of power in the building, the manager's residence.

Sitting at my makeshift desk—a door propped up on wooden horses—I flipped through Don in 302's lease and didn't find a phone number or emergency contact listed. Ours would be face-to-face encounters. I also discovered that the Solipsist's given name was Marie De Luca.

I fired up the laptop. I was facing a blank wall, on purpose. There'd be no pictures or affirmations to distract me. I'd simply lay down a steady stream of words until I slipped a rubber band around a completed manuscript.

I was thirty-eight, at the peak of my creative powers. Only, I had nothing to write about. There wasn't a single incident, like helping a friend dispose of a dead body, to build on. And no inspiration from looking at the blank wall. Then again, Leonardo da Vinci used the cracks in a wall to spark his creativity. My walls were freshly re-plastered, smooth, without any history. I walked around the apartment, using movement as a way to stimulate my imagination. Ten minutes went by, twenty ...

I had it! I'd use a frame of reference, my favorite writer: Charles Bukowski. Each of his books covered a phase of his life. He had four books. I only needed one.

Buk, as his friends and sycophants called him, began with *Post Office*. He was around fifty then, mentally and physically shot from his dozen or so years as a mail carrier, then sorter. The three weeks of abuse hurled upon me by spinster paralegals while I was sorting mail at the entertainment law firm of Ginsberg and Schnapp was a pale comparison.

Next up for Buk was *Factotum*, covering his wanderings across America, drifting from dead-end job to dead-end job, livened up with trips to the racetrack, back-alley brawls, and a string of relationships with deranged, alcoholic women.

This was a promising path. Clearly, I was in a *Factotum* stage of my life, right now! I was living it, in the present tense.

I'd open with the first in a string of jobs I'd held, threading my way to the Resident Manager role. That'd be the backbone, the spine I'd use to attach the muscles, tendons and sinews. But I wasn't writing and submitting short stories and poems like Buk. Or drinking, going to the track, on the dole, shacked up with a crazed broad ... Hmm: There were no vices for me to mine.

Angling back in the Herman Miller Aeron-chair I'd snagged off the street and wheeled to the trunk of my 1978 mimosa-yellow Mercedes, I pondered starting a prostitution ring in the building to generate material. While I was working out the details in my head, I noticed a water stain on the ceiling above my desk. It was fresh, because water was pooling around it.

I did not panic. But I moved quickly to secure the laptop from potential water damage and hard drive ruin. It was now safe on the kitchen table. With barely a hesitation, I shrewdly spread my three least-favorite water-repellant raincoats over the hardwood floor to prevent it from warping, thus safeguarding the owner's property.

As Resident Manager, vested with full powers to call in workmen—as I saw fit—I consulted *the* vendor list. It listed workmen for every job and/or calamity imaginable, including: pressure washing, downed power lines, peepholes, asphalt repairs/seal coating, shower/tub glazing, etc. It was three pages long—in eight-point font! They were all at my disposal! I dialed Herman the plumber.

"Herman, it's Rupert. The new manager at 1105 Kedge Road ..."

"Yes, sir ... yes, sir ..." He sounded harried, out of breath. Like a man had been sent to kill him, a struggle was in progress, and now that man was reaching for the gun Herman had knocked out of his hand, while he repeatedly smashed the guy's forearm against his desk. And Herman had an arm wrapped around the guy's waist, holding him back in an ever-so-tenuous grip, OR ... he was just really busy.

"There's water leaking from my ceiling ..."

"Can I come right over, sir?"

Wow! I wouldn't have to wait until I was knee-deep in water, setting up a bucket brigade with any and all available tenants, dumping water onto the parched, yellowish lawn out front.

"Perfect. I'm in 204."

In what seemed like a matter of moments, the buzzer rang. This guy was good. Elated, I raced down to meet Herman and hold the front door open for him. Profusely sweating from the battle with his would-be killer—or record-breaking sprint from La Crescenta to Glendale—Herman lugged a huge metal tool case and electric saw up the stairs.

"Need a hand?"

"No ... thank you, sir. Thank you."

Herman's politeness was overwhelming. I was used to L.A. waitresses who wanted to spit on me for having the audacity to ask them to bring a bottle of ketchup to the table. Something they'd clearly forgotten for a burger and fries.

Not Herman. He unfurled a heavy-duty tarp over my desk, trumping the trilogy of foul-weather wear strewn across the floor. Eyeing the water now coursing down the wall, Herman turned, grim.

"What is it?" I braced myself to collapse in Herman's arms, if the news was truly bad.

"We have to cut through the wall."

I was lightheaded, dizzy. "When can you start?"

"Now. You'll need to let the tenants know that we're going to have to shut the water off."

"For how long?"

"Two ... three hours."

I wondered how that would go over.

After posting a notice inside the lobby door and above the mailboxes, I went from apartment to apartment, knocking on doors. No one was home. Or, they were performing lewd acts behind closed doors and needed their privacy. Hopefully, running water wasn't a part of the show.

Only Marie opened her door.

"Will there be noise?" Her dead shark eyes betrayed enough emotion to show displeasure at the sight of me.

"He's using an electric saw."

"I NEED to catch up on my paperwork."

"It can't be helped."

"Did you post notices by the side entrances? You'd better. Not everyone comes in through the front door."

"Good idea."

I followed Marie's instructions to the letter.

Heading back to my apartment, guided by the sound of saw to plaster, I ran into a mid-40's woman clutching my plumbing notice in a tight fist. She had a severe bob haircut (with bangs), pale makeup, a fashion-forward outfit, and bordering-on-clownish red lipstick. I suppose she thought it was attractive. It made me anxious.

"This is unclear." She waved it in my face.

"What do you mean?"

"You wrote it in paragraph form."

"And?" I stared at her, not sure where she was going with this.

"Wouldn't it make more sense to put the information in sub-headings: "Who, what, when, where, why ...?"

"Yeah ..."

"Good. And I need that plumber to look at my tub, before he tries to leave." She held out a long-fingered hand. "I'm Judy. 305."

"Rupert ..."

We shook.

"I know who you are."

"What gave me away?"

"Aside from Larry's description, the worry in your eyes, and Sharpie in your hand matching the print on the plumbing notes ... shall I go on?"

"You have an eye for detail."

"You think?"

Inside my apartment, Herman was on his hands and knees cleaning the hardwood floors, the hole in the wall meticulously sealed off with heavy-duty plastic from lethal spiders, poisonous snakes, decomposing bodies and whatever or whoever was lurking behind the wall. A brand-new section of pipe gleamed through the plastic.

"I can do that Herman."

"Thank you, sir. It's no problem."

Uncomfortable about sitting down while Herman scrubbed the floor, even if I was engaged in MENTAL work, I occupied myself doing dishes and making my bed.

"All done, sir." Herman was by the front door, a bucket filled with dirty rags, the floor sparkling.

"Do you have time to look at 305? It's a tub issue."

"Absolutely ..."

Judy opened her door. Stood there, a green-tinged cocktail in her free hand. Absinthe? Crème de menthe? A Midori sour?

"What's the problem, ma'am?" Herman asked.

"It's the tub back there. It takes forever. I'm sure you've seen one before."

We trod down a wood-paneled entranceway, stacks of books on the floor, to a pink-tiled bathroom. Herman knelt down and ran the hot and cold full-bore, waited. A vortex took the water down to the center of the earth.

"See ... it's slow." Judy proclaimed.

Herman looked at me for an explanation. I had none.

"What about the valve stems?" I arched my eyebrows at Herman.

Picking up on my clue, while Judy peered down at him, Herman turned the faucet handles, jiggled the insides, and then tightened them with a screwdriver.

"They weren't seated right. Now it should be fine." Again, he let the water run full-bore. Another vortex sucked the water down at multiple g-forces.

"Good?" I looked at Judy.

She used a long-nailed finger to twirl the ice in her glass. "I suppose."

Out in the hallway, Herman advised me. "I don't trust her."

If Herman didn't trust her, I wouldn't trust her. Not that I knew why.

I was starting to think about getting the hole in my wall patched, when I heard the sound of a postal truck's cargo door slam shut. I flew to the mailboxes, anticipating an offer of marriage from a Russian mail-order bride, a time-capsule letter from a World War II pilot to his sweetheart back home, who had once lived in my apartment, or bills. Receiving mail was the highlight of my day.

Hiding on the first-floor landing, peering at the Filipina mail carrier slotting the mail, anxiously waiting for her to finish so I could get at it, I spotted a gorgeous Eurasian outside, fumbling in her bag. She was flanked by what I assumed was her boyfriend. He bore a familial resemblance to some of the Orcs in *The Lord of the Rings*. I wondered if he lived close by, or had made the long journey from Middle-earth. No more than five-three or five-three and a quarter, he'd pumped his body up to freakish proportions and came complete with a sloping brow and beady eyes. Even from across the lobby, I could see the tufts of hair on his knuckles.

I was thankful the Orc contained his Orcian tendencies and wasn't ripping the huge antique door off its hinges while the Eurasian continued to dig in the depths of her enormous purse, fishing for keys. To mitigate the Orc's running amok in the building, leaving a trail of carnage in his wake, I nonchalantly crossed past the mail carrier and opened the door for them.

"Thanks, you must be the new manager."

"Yes, Rupert."

"I'm Maybelline."

I nodded to the boyfriend, who looked right through me.

Finally fishing her keys out—buried amongst what I imagined were condom wrappers and a pair of furry handcuffs—in actuality Maybelline pulled out some ratty tissues and a half-open roll of LifeSavers.

After we all got our mail, we awkwardly negotiated heading up the stairs. The Orc let Maybelline go first, positioning his body between me and her, as if I'd been crowding her, hoping to cop a feel or finger her en route. I wasn't like that. But, if Maybelline came around to my apartment after the Orc made the journey back to Middle-earth, confided in me that the Orc and she were on the outs, needed consoling, and ended up fucking me, I'd be okay with that.

"Rupert, there's water leaking from my bathroom ceiling," Maybelline told me.

Was plumbing the Achilles heel of the Dryden Arms?

"Hmm ... can I take a look?"

I could tell the Orc didn't like that idea.

"I need to see who I should call."

"Sure ..."

Entering Maybelline's apartment, it was better than I could have imagined. There was a four-poster bed that took up the bulk of Maybelline's living room, racks of sexy clothes, a small worktable with a sewing machine and piles of high-heeled boots. As soon as I could draw my attention to it, I saw an all-too-familiar water stain on the bathroom ceiling.

"I'm gonna need to call the plumber." Herman, my new best friend.

The Orc gnashed his teeth at the impending intrusion. Maybelline looked stressed.

Herman sounded much calmer this time. The death-struggle with his would-be attacker must have been resolved in his favor. Using his acute powers of deduction, Herman suggested I call in the handyman Vasco, and check the roof.

I had to get a plan in place quickly, as the Orc looked ready to gut me if I didn't get out of there soon. We coordinated for me to let Vasco in, later that day when they were out. I found their lack of suspicion curious, given the trouble I could get into in their absence. That boot collection was too good to ignore.

Focusing on writing now was out of the question. I had to stay mentally prepared for the arrival of Vasco. He showed up three hours late. No explanation.

Hispanic, portly, deep into middle age, he was either drunk or possessed a naturally jovial disposition. He'd brought a "helper," as he called him: Cortez, a little guy with alert eyes who appeared to speak zero English.

I was eyeing Maybelline's boots, while Vasco checked out the water stain. He and Cortez started talking about something in Spanish, and I'm pretty sure I heard the word *cerveza* discussed.

We divided and conquered. Cortez peeled off from us and fearlessly crawled into the attic. Vasco and I hit the stairs. The nine steps up to the roof completely drained him. Topside, he was dripping sweat and breathing heavily.

Cortez reappeared and reported his findings. After a significant and rapid-fire exchange, I noticed the word *la lima* had been prominently featured.

Cortez went straight to work on the drainage pipes. Vasco headed over there and assumed a supervisory stance. But he was in fact just staring off in the distance, a giant smile plastered on his face. I wanted to ask him what the secret to his happiness was, or what brand of liquor he had coursing through his veins.

Cortez was on to something. He brought us both to an AC unit. I stood by while further discussion occurred.

"It's the air-condition ... yes ... it needs cover." Vasco told me. "Cortez fix *Sábado.*"

"And the hole in my wall ..."

"*Sábado.*"

Cortez nodded. "Si."

DATE	TRANSACTION DESCRIPTION	PAYMENT, FEE, WITHDRAWAL (-)	✓	DEPOSIT, CREDIT (+)	$
12.1.14	Lean Cuisines, smaller-sized key chain ring, aluminum foil	96.12			3,422.68
12.1.14	Unemployment (two weeks)			900.00	4,322.68

5

Like all the greats, I'd call on my innate sense of discipline. When I set my mind to something, I was unstoppable. In line with Buk, I'd use the cold light of day—when things are in proportion and lucidity reigns—to write. Buk worked nights at the Terminal Annex Post Office. I was free to sleep and rest my mind so each morning I'd be fresh and ready to "lay down the line," as Buk called it.

First though, I had to get the environment right. Recreating the atmosphere of Buk's east Hollywood courtyard apartment wouldn't quite work. There weren't bags of empties piled everywhere from constant drinking (I didn't drink), soiled underwear lying around (I was neat), or broken windows from bottles hurled by tweaked girlfriends (I was single).

I sifted deeper. Like Buk, I was in a precarious financial situation. Good. Unemployment would quickly run out. Better. Then again, I didn't pay rent. No pressure there. Good in theory, bad for my purposes.

Girlfriends. I didn't have one. Maybe I should have one. What did that say about me? I was normal. Even heard myself referred to as charming once in a while. Although weird also came up. Buk juggled any number of women. Not all hags either, as cohorts in his novels called them, but also strippers, prostitutes, loose women ... pure chaos. No wonder he had a strict writing schedule.

I had standards. Meth-heads, Craigslist freaks and the like were out. If, on the other hand, a psychiatrist/prostitute were available, that'd be ideal. Actually, even a psychologist-or-MFT/prostitute would be fine.

Let's see: Buk was a six-footer; I wasn't. Not my fault, but still a disadvantage with women. Looks: pleasant, with a baby-face, not pock-marked like Buk's from the remnants of acne vulgaris. Intelligence: high. A match. Eyesight: poor. I wore glasses, sometimes contacts. Buk hadn't worn either. Although, maybe his eyesight was bad and he eschewed wearing prosthetics of any kind.

Booze was almost the entire basis of Buk's existence. I only drank coffee, which didn't have the same mythology. The vibe was different. I was looking for exactitude, not verisimilitude.

Classical music: hated it. Buk tuned his radio to a classical music station whenever he wrote. The racetrack was also a non-starter. It was Buk's escape. I had an allergic reaction to cigarette, cigar and pot smoke emitted by the assorted cretins and drunken thieves that frequented the track.

I was still deep in thought, establishing links with Buk, when a more pressing issue occurred to me. Were there any Lean Cuisines left, for lunch? If so, what kind? And then there was Marie. Not wanting to risk an encounter without having a full plan formulated for the creaking floorboards, it was time for a return trip to Don's apartment.

Waiting for him to open up, I went through a few cycles of the *Jeopardy* theme song. Hearing him shuffle around his apartment, I wondered if I needed to set up camp in the corridor, and get the franks & beans started. I finally heard him maneuver several bolts, chains, latches and an eyehook.

I was semi-shocked to see Don standing there wearing a skimpy, ratty towel around his waist, exposing a bony frame. Don didn't seem at all self-conscious. But I was. Since he wasn't at all wet, he hadn't come out of the shower. Could he be spearheading an elder nudist collective? Was he busy working on the newsletter? I hoped there weren't photos involved, and that he wouldn't ask me to assist.

"Sorry to bother you, but Marie ..."

Don had no reaction.

"... the woman who lives downstairs ..." Still nothing.

As we stood facing one another, his towel thankfully still in place, I was free to notice the environs. There were a number of framed portraits of film noir stars on a kidney-shaped desk, a wing chair with the bottom busted out, and a spectacular view of the mountains.

So, if I killed Don and took his apartment it'd be nice. I'd spend my days taking in the scenic mountains and breathing revitalizing foothill air. But even with his bony physique, Don looked like he could be scrappy. Killing him might not prove so easy. The elderly can be surprisingly agile. I'd wind up not getting any writing done anyway. I'd let it go.

"The floorboards are creaking and it's really bothering her."

Already seeming to understand the problem, Don knelt down on the floor, which drastically increased my fear of towel slippage. I was spared. Although, a bit more upper thigh was revealed than I really wanted to see.

Don raised a section of threadbare carpet, showing me that it wasn't tacked down. "It's loose."

"Yeah."

"You're going to have to replace the floorboards, or put down some thicker carpeting."

It sounded good to me, and might appease Marie. I helped Don up, so he could at least have one hand free to keep that towel rock-steady. We had options.

Once I sorted out the particulars, I'd deliver the good news to Marie. I would have to consult the trusty vendor list. But I didn't want to give any more business to carpet/vinyl guys who no doubt lived on mini-Versailles estates.

Tradesmen always made a killing. The histories are replete with tales of their good fortune: the men who outfitted ships with barrels, sails and whatnot; pick-axe and tin-pan suppliers during the 1849 Gold Rush; into the modern-era with car mechanics who drove $100,000 BMWs. I rued the liberal arts education that had left me an unskilled polymath, poor and without a trade.

I'd bundle jobs. Have Vasco deal with the carpet and hole in my wall. But I'd deal with him later. I had a more pressing issue to attend to. I had to do some laundry, having already reversed my underwear too many times for comfort. I stuffed a pile of dirty clothes in a laundry bag, slung it over my shoulder like a sailor headed to sea, and descended to the basement.

One of the keys Larry had provided opened the laundry machine coin boxes. For my entire tenure at the building, I'd be spared the expense of using my own quarters. It was a perk. I opened a coin box, stacked some quarters, and slid five into the slots. Water seeped into washer #1, and I was off to the races. Precisely twenty-six minutes later, I transferred clothes to dryer #1. I now had forty-five minutes, thirty-five of which would be used masturbating on my kidney-shaped chair, giving me ten to get back downstairs, preventing any tenants from making off with my freshly dried clothes.

The dryer cycle eventually having completed, the clothes remained damp. Fuck! I slotted another five quarters to finish the job. But ten minutes in, the fucker stopped. I tried opening and closing the dryer door, seeing if I could get it to restart; checked if the plug was loose; looked for a magical re-set button; chanted ... nothing.

In desperation, I might have to use the tenement-like clothesline by the garages, putting my wardrobe at risk for a Dr. Richard Kimble–type theft.

Instead, I left a message for the laundry repair guy and opted to drape my clothes across chairs, the shower curtain rod, doorknobs, drawer pulls, etc. As I hung the last of my Fruit of the Looms on the bedroom doorknob, there was an insistent knocking at the door. You'd think by the ferocity/impatience, I was moving at Don the towel man's pace.

It was Brenda. I felt the bile rising up my throat.

"The dryer's not working."

"Yeah. I called it in."

"How could you? It just broke."

"It actually broke on me." I pointed out the moist Fruit of the Looms.

Mikey zoomed past, doing suicides.

"Then where's the sign, Rupert?"

"Putting finishing touches on it now. Want to proofread it for me?"

She didn't know what to make of that. Was I mocking her, or genuinely wanting her disabled dryer note feedback?

Ignoring me. "When will it be fixed?"

"I'm waiting for a callback from the repairman."

"That's not good enough."

"There is still one that works."

"I don't have all day to do laundry."

"You can use the Laundromat down the street."

"I'm not leaving the building."

"Okay."

"This is ridiculous." She stalked off.

Needing a reprieve, I took a short walk to the local coffee shop on Brand Boulevard, the main Glendale artery. I had already drifted past a Korean dry cleaner, a church, a Korean salad bar place, a stationery store, another Korean dry cleaner, a Korean barbershop and a Korean shoe repair, when my phone rang in front of a kosher butcher. It was Larry, no doubt on a break from his medical experiments.

"I hear we're having a little problem in the laundry room."

"I left a message for the repair guy. How'd you hear about it?"

"Brenda tells me you're not on top of things."

"I don't know how much more on top I can be, calling the repair guy ninety seconds after it broke down."

"She said you told her to take her laundry down the street."

"It was a suggestion."

Larry sighed. We were surprisingly simpatico, even though I was a Jew. He knew I was on the frontlines.

"There's one more thing."

I let my diaphragm fill with air.

"Marie wants you to start taking in her

newspaper."

I released it. As much as I wanted to use Marie's paper for kindling and set her on fire, I told Larry it was no problem.

The last obstacle between me and a simple cup of coffee was a beefy, stadium-security-type guy barreling toward me. When he got closer, I realized it was the tenant from 106. Clutching a coffee in a catcher's-mitt-sized hand, he stopped right in front of me. Now, granted we were in Southern California, by this early December date, it was chilly by most people's standards. But this guy wore shorts, flip-flops, a faded "Saturday Night Live EST. 1977" T-shirt and slicked-back hair.

He dispensed with formalities. "Don't put a name on my mailbox. People keep looking me up."

"Really. Why?"

"Magic tricks."

"You're a magician?"

"A PROFESSIONAL magician."

"I'm a writer."

"Of what?"

"I'm exploring themes for a novel."

"Sounds like a crock."

"It's all preparation. Like painting a room. First you spread a tarp, tape off ..."

He jabbed a thick finger in my chest. "Start the fucking novel." He bulled his way past me.

When I ducked inside the coffee shop, Don was at the counter asking a heavyset Armenian woman, with breasts so large one of her bra cups would easily fit over my entire head, if the wrapped pastry in his hand was a day old. She looked annoyed, grabbed it from Don, and rang it up.

She was no better with me. But Heavyset's looks of disgust and slow-motion process of pouring me a coffee were worth it; the Armenian brew was delicious.

Taking my beverage outside, I saw Don seated at a vinyl-checked table. He was delicately shredding and eating his pastry. I'd felt bad for his rough treatment at the hands of Heavyset and wanted to offer him company, a form of solace. I asked Don to join him.

He seemed more nervous fully clothed, so I made sure not to make any sudden movements. Still unsure, Don moved his pastry plate closer. I took it as a yes, and sat down.

"I'll call and let you know when Vasco can come by."

Matter-of-factly. "I don't have a telephone."

Since we didn't have a Morse code system set up between us, I offered to slide a note under his door. He liked that idea.

"Let me ask you something. Could you tell me what a Web site is?"

As far as I knew, Don hadn't recently emerged from a bomb shelter or been the stateside equivalent of a Japanese soldier who'd fought on Iwo Jima and stayed in a cave network years after the war had ended, not getting the news. And we were going on two decades of the Internet being a part of people's everyday lives. Then again, if Alexander Graham Bell's invention wasn't a part of Don's world, I supposed the Internet would have been out of the question.

"Well ... first off ... you would need a computer." I took a chance he'd know what that meant. He seemed to follow my line of thinking. I went on to explain that all computers now had access to information via something called the Internet. You could simply type in the name of a Web site, and be transported to anything and everything you could imagine, globally. Don looked at me like I'd just told him the biggest bullshit story ever. Fucking with his head further, I hit him with Wikipedia, G-mail and eBay and went in for the kill with OkCupid.com.

Looking at Don in his dismay, I remembered a lit professor telling me about being in France at the end of World War II when word came of the atom bomb destroying Hiroshima, and how it'd sounded like science fiction, one bomb decimating an entire city. But the Internet had been a gradual thing. It hadn't appeared overnight. What had been preoccupying Don, that he hadn't noticed any of this?

I started to become preoccupied by that bear claw of his. Don must have seen me eyeing it, and offered me a piece.

It was a nice gesture, but there was no telling if Don had washed his hands before picking it apart.

"I'm good. Thanks." But not really. I thought about getting my own.

"Those hillsides were free of homes when I first moved here."

"When was that?"

"'55."

"You from here?"

"Illinois."

"Chicago?" I immediately got excited thinking of deep-dish pizza.

Don looked uncomfortable. "A farm outside the city."

"Where'd you live, when you first got here?"

"I was homeless."

The man sitting across from me was the

manifestation of my innermost fear and anxiety: ending up on the streets, a plastic cup in one of my arthritic hands, reaching out for spare change when I was well into my 70s. My parents having passed away, and my being an only child without an extended family, homelessness always felt like a very real possibility. I'd been working without a financial safety net for a while. More blocks of time would pass, jobs, friends ... everything was fragile.

Spooked, it was time to go. Glad my laundry was comped.

DATE	TRANSACTION DESCRIPTION	PAYMENT, FEE, WITHDRAWAL (-)	✓	DEPOSIT, CREDIT (+)	$
12.2.14				15 quarters	3.75
12.2.14		15 quarters – lost			4,322.68
12.2.14	Coffee, bear claw	2.63			4,320.05

6

The morning after the shooting, I had some post-attempted-homicide items to deal with. Most importantly, checking on Eli's whereabouts and current status on the L.A. County Vine Program. Spooner, the slovenly detective, had clued me into the victims of violent crimes Web site to give me a heads up in case Eli was out and had thoughts of finishing the job. Bail was set at $1.2 million. That was steep. I should be safe. Eli didn't have that kind of money. Or did he? After all, I hadn't known he was a homicidal lunatic. Perhaps the modest appearance of things in his apartment was just a charade. For all I knew, in addition to his now transparent homicidal tendencies Eli might be part of a vast meth ring and have access to large sums of cash on- and offshore.

I was worked up. But I still had to call Larry and gave him a run-down of last night's events. Larry was as cool as Gregory Peck's Josef Mengele in *The Boys from Brazil.* He patched us in with Duncan Danforth. In an effort to make sure no blame was directed at me, I reminded them both that Eli had been in the building long before I arrived.

"Eviction's in process." Larry announced.

"Rupert, what's the mood in the building?" Duncan asked.

"I've calmed the waters." I was always happy to bring a nautical term into any conversation related to the building.

"Good. Larry, stay on the line. Thanks for handling everything, Rupert."

"No problem." I assumed they'd discuss further ramifications of the shooting, or commiserate as to why Marie or Brenda had been spared. You'd think they'd have been the first ones targeted. I'd never know.

When I called to check on Jonas, post-traumatic stress disorder hadn't set in and he wasn't at an undisclosed location speaking on a burn phone; as a precaution in case Eli's meth-head friends had rounded up the $1.2 million, the Vine program hadn't been updated, and Eli was closing in on him. Rather, Jonas and Magellan were out shopping for decorative throw pillows and a new lampshade.

As the day wore on, I became like Bukowski in his east Hollywood courtyard apartment, but instead of people dropping by with beer and wine or groupies offering sex, they brought tales from the night of the shooting.

"It's all about life condition," the Magician explained. He propped himself up—Buddha-like—on the apartment's prime piece of furniture, a kidney-shaped chair I'd done a wild U-turn for on La Cienega Boulevard, a.k.a. The Swamp. I'd leapt from the mimosa-yellow Mercedes, raced to the dealer with bills flapping in the tornado I was generating, á la Storm from *X-Men*, then drove away with it secured on top of my car. Thus beginning my love affair with unique home furnishings.

The Magician arched back in comfort on this special piece, while I sat rigid and upright on a less-favored straight-backed chair. "He's been swayed by the eight winds."

I contemplated his words. "I thought there were only four. Interesting."

"You have to understand, Rupert," he emphasized. "This is an unenlightened man."

"A felon now." I noted.

"Only in this life, Rupert."

"You believe in Karma?"

"All Buddhists do."

"I've gone to Buddhist meetings."

"So you understand, Rupert. This is Eli working out issues from a past life."

"In jail." I chimed in.

The Magician stood up, surveying my almost breathtaking view. "Too bad, you're one floor away from Don's million-dollar view."

"He's lived up there forever. He's not going anywhere."

"The man's old. He's gotta go sometime." The Magician turned to face me. Made significant eye contact. "Don't bother calling the security company. I'll reprogram the front door code. You know that's one of my hobbies? I dabble in security."

"That means what?"

"I can do it for you, but it's gonna cost you."

"What are we talking here?"

The Magician pondered his worth, and hit me with it.

"A hundred and twenty quarters for laundry."

So laundry was his game. It made sense. He was a big, sweaty kind of fellow. Probably had to change his *SNL* T-shirts three times a day. I could see where that would get expensive. In any event, the offer was a lot more time and cost-effective than calling in the security company.

"We have a deal," I told him.

"I can also change the locks and cut new keys for all the tenants."

Was there no end to this man's hobbies?

While I did have concerns about an illegal key-cutting operation, I figured what the hell. I'd let it go and keep the quarters flowing.

Twelve more loads of laundry later, we had a deal and I'd be flush with keys.

After the Magician left, I went and stared out the window. Wondered. Could Don's fading senses even appreciate his view? I—possessed of all my senses—had to suffer a view obstructed by trees one floor below. It hardly seemed fair.

I could lure Don to the free tennis courts on Verdugo. Tell him I'm looking for a new partner. Would hit some balls right to him, given the likelihood he couldn't run anymore. Tout the health benefits. Set his mind at ease. Then, strategically place balls just outside Don's reach, stretching his plaque-hardened arteries to the breaking point, adding undue stress to his heart. I'd offer to drive. We'd play a set, drive off, loop back to the courts, and pretending we'd just arrived, play again. If Don seemed aware of my ploy, I'd feign ignorance and trade on the elderly's notorious short-term memory loss and say we hadn't played yet. If he thought we had, we'd laugh it off and hit the courts. Then I'd finish him off once and for all.

I'd ask Larry for Don's place. It was a single. They'd get more for my one-bedroom. But if for some reason things didn't pan out, after Don's death, at the very least I'd snag his kidney-shaped desk, as a complementary piece to my kidney-shaped chair.

NO! I wasn't a killer. Only been in one fight my whole life, helping out a second-grade buddy who'd been jumped by two other kids. That one didn't end in bloodshed, just a trip to the principal's office.

It was the Magician's fault! He'd influenced me, raving about the view from Don's apartment. I would do no harm unto Don.

That settled, and having put the Eli situation to bed, I was free to start writing. Fingers poised over the laptop keys, I was ready to transmit the words of God through his vessel on Earth, in this case me. An hour went by. Nothing happened. But I knew what to do. I'd unlock the universe with a simple phrase: *Nam myo renge kyo.*

A cute girl had approached me at the beach and told me that if I said these words, I'd access my highest life condition and achieve enlightenment. I'd be plugged directly into the power of the universe. All I had to do was chant this one phrase and the universe would be at my disposal.

At the time, all I wanted was to fuck that cute girl. I managed to get a great parking spot later that day, but no sex. Now, I had to put my positive energy into the novel. I went to the kidney-shaped chair to chant. In mere moments, a torrent of words would spill onto the page.

I let loose: *Nam myo renge kyo* ... over and over again, the words resonating in my head. I grew worried. Would I inadvertently conjure up something unearthly? Not a black hole, I didn't have Large Hadron Collider levels of voltage to cause a cataclysmic event, but maybe visions of ... what? The Buddha, God, a gateway to a parallel universe? Or the Silver Surfer, guided by my voice, might bring Galactus to drain the Earth of its energy. I'd cross that bridge when I came to it.

Mind in a Buddha-like state, I honed in on Buk's *Ham on Rye* as the novel that most closely resembled my own experiences. How, though, had Buk, looking back more than fifty years, remembered conversations and details so clearly? He was a drunk. His head battered in by a series of back-alley brawls. A true mystery.

I didn't drink or take drugs, yet only had fragments of memories. Was I a robot? Like in Philip K. Dick's story *The Electric Ant*, where Poole's experience of the world is encoded on a tape reel inside his body? Or could I be the missing android Harrison Ford was chasing in *Blade Runner*? The critically acclaimed adaptation of a Dick novel turned into a box office bonanza and cult classic. In any case, there was no way I'd be able to delve more than ten, fifteen years into my past. Extended hypnotherapy sessions? That would mean shopping for a good hypnotist. COBRA probably didn't cover it.

My concentration was broken by the sound of something sliding under my door. It was a note, unsigned. No envelope. My name didn't appear anywhere on it.

ACTUAL NOTE LEFT UNDER DOOR:

To Whom It Concerns

you take advantage and park here to

often, emergency's, understand we all

might need to park here at times.

Also the garage belongs to a tenant

here, so please do not treat this as

a parking spot. When you lock your

car and beep it you disturb us in our

bedrooms. Thank you for minding this.

Right off the bat, I noticed the disregard this

person had for presentation. It was written on a piece of lined paper torn in half. Not neatly torn in half, where you fold the paper one way, then the other, for a crisp cut. This piece of paper had jagged edges at the top. The other peculiarity was, even on this approximately half-sheet of paper, the writing started three-quarters down the page. Had something been written on the top half of the page? Why not start with a fresh sheet of paper?

There was also the poor grammar. "To" instead of "too," "emergency's" instead of "emergencies," a comma missing after "Also." Other missing commas, the first sentence starting in lower case. But the final phrase was unique: "Thank you for minding this."

The handwriting was peculiar too. Large letters, which a handwriting analyst I had paid $15 along the Venice boardwalk said meant boldness. I was bold. This person was bold; there was common ground.

I slid the note into a plastic sleeve, preserving it as evidence. Who knew if I'd ever have to testify about the circumstances surrounding it? I was placing the note in a folder marked Dryden Arms, when there was a rapping on the door.

"She leave a note?" Hat Guy was all business.

"Who?"

"Brenda."

"How do you know?"

"Dude. I've seen her at it. It's her frickin' hobby. She's got nothing better to do."

"I read it. Want me to talk to her?"

He waved me off. "Here's the irony, the short, fat bitch takes up two spaces with HER giant Caddie. You know she's using her garage as storage space. Totally illegal."

"Larry told me to let it go. She's too much of a

nightmare. No one wants to go near that."

"Right." He rolled his eyes. "Anyway, I'm not blocking anyone. I'm loading my vans. Have you heard her cat meowing? I bet she didn't get permission to bring that thing in the building."

With absolutely no transition or connective, conversational tissue, Hat Guy forged on.

"Astrid spoke to Eli after he fired the shots. She asked him what he was doing. And told him, 'Eli. You can't do that, Eli. Eli, you can't do that.' Like he's a child. She even saw the gun in his hand. It had a yellow handle. Guess she's gonna have to testify."

"All Marie cared about was her no scent-policy. I'm surprised she didn't make me hose down the SWAT team before they stormed the premises."

"That's called deviation, man. She's reverting to the norm."

"I just thought she was a phobic lunatic."

"Back in the day ..."

"What day was that?"

Hat Guy paused.

"... the FBI-training I got ... bet you didn't know that about me."

"I didn't."

"I'm a master of human behavior."

"Really?"

"I'm very observant. Details DO NOT escape me." Except for the fact we'd had a crazed would-be killer in our midst. That particular detail had escaped Hat Guy.

He was on to the next. "We need to get those gardeners from across the street. De Soto's for shit."

"Duncan won't allow it."

"That's bullshit. The lawn is turning YELLOW."

"We can only use the sprinklers twice a week with the drought."

"Then we have got to go with a desert theme and tear out the grass. I can do it."

"That's not gonna happen."

Shaking his head. "It looks bad out there."

"Not my call."

After an uncomfortable silence, Hat Guy shook his stetson'd head and trudged off.

Not wanting any more gunfire in the hallways, I figured I should call Brenda re: the note.

"Hey, Brenda. It's Rupe ..."

"Why is he so selfish?" She interrupted. "He thinks it's his own private loading zone back there. What? He's not strong enough to carry his own stupid pictures, artwork or whatever those hideous lacquered things are out to the street?"

My phone dinged with a text.

Judy (1/3): There's smoke in my apartment. Well at least it's residual cigarette and marijuana smoke from that pothead, self-absorbed narcissist Jonas. He cracked Eli but not me. And that patchouli incense doesn't fool anyone.

End text bubble. Brenda continued.

"It's like we live in a ghetto. Did you know he takes up three full spaces on the street ... THREE ..."

I wonder what it was about the number three that made a neighborhood a ghetto. I hadn't realized two was the cutoff.

My phone dinged again. Judy (2/3): When's the dryer getting fixed?

Me: Waiting for a call back.

Judy: Stay on them.

End text bubble. Brenda continued.

"... I should move out of here. This used to be a nice building. Neighbors were considerate. Selfish prick."

Speaking of selfish, I thought it odd that Brenda didn't stop to mention the shooting.

My phone dinged again. Judy (3/3): You need to get up here and smell this. I'm choking.

End text bubble. Brenda continued.

"... he thinks he's so cool with his hats. Who gives a fuck? I try to be kind. Can I just tell you? When I think about how the rest of us have to drive around looking for a parking space, because asshole Hat Guy ..."

Brenda went on for a bit longer and eventually tired herself out. I went to 305.

"Who's there?" Judy asked when I knocked on her door, even though I was standing dead center of her peephole.

"It's Rupert ..."

She flung the door open. "It's just ... smoke is a carcinogen ... and this is a non-smoking building ..."

At this point 206 was incarcerated, 305 (Judy) perilously close to lung cancer, and who knew what other tenants sharing common walls with Jonas were repressing their hostilities. "I'll remind him."

"I know he was almost killed. But Jonas owes me respect. If it wasn't for me, he wouldn't be working for that other stupid, gay prick."

"I'll take care of it."

"And what's up with the dryer?"

"In progress."

"I want a date, Rupert."

Was she asking me out, or wanting to know when the dryer would be drying her clothes again?

"Ah ..."

"There's a lack of amenities here to begin with. Come in ..."

Stepping over stacks of fiction books scattered across the floor, I followed Judy from the entranceway to the living room and stood admiring her near-Don-spectacular view.

"This living room is cramped. It's like being sardined on a New York City subway car. There's no built in shelving. I have a drink cart in here, because the kitchen isn't big enough. I need more counter space, a bigger refrigerator."

She must like to cook. I wonder if she makes pancakes or crepes. I like pancakes. Thin ones with old-fashioned syrup. Have that gluten allergy. Dairy's bad too.

"You know I can hear the sirens from the firehouse night and day. And the kids who live over there—she pointed a malevolent finger like the Wicked Witch of the West toward the backyard of a house beyond the living room window—"are constantly on their swing set. I can hear the springs creak."

Running low on dental floss. Is it worth a trip to the store? Get a multi-pack next time. Vitamins. I should take some. C. My throat's been scratchy. What else?

"The A/C is barely adequate. It doesn't even touch the bathroom."

So Pluto is definitely not a planet. What then? A

dwarf planet? Lifeless rock leftover from the formation of the solar system? The New Horizons spacecraft will clear things up. CVS has shoelaces. The right one on my Nikes is frayed. What are those things on the end called again? Eyelets are the holes on the shoes. Not sure.

"Would it be too much to ask for a garbage disposal?"

Wouldn't need to drive to CVS. It's an easy enough walk. No parking hassles. Try a Cronut. Hazelnut.

"You're a good listener, Rupert. It's refreshing in a man."

"Oh ... okay. I'll head over to Jonas's now." Judy walked me to the door. Opening it, I looked back at her. She considered me. Flicked my hair. It made me uncomfortable.

In the hallway, it was silent as a tomb. Ever since the shooting, tenants were very conscious about keeping the noise down.

I knocked on Jonas's door, opposite Judy's, and felt a wave of energy headed toward me. Jonas practically tore the door off its hinges.

"What now, Rupert?"

"Ah ... Judy texted me ..."

"Jesus, I left my garbage outside the door for a couple hours ..."

Jonas inadvertently incriminated himself with yet another thoughtless act. I'm sure it was a thrill for the entire third floor to get a whiff of his rotting trash.

"It's not about that."

"Oh ..."

"It's the smoking, Jonas. Cigarettes, pot ..."

"Tell Miss Cocktail Party I have a medical

license." Was it to cure his pathological lack of consideration of others? Apparently, Jonas wasn't worried about another attempt on his life.

"You're gonna have to take it outside."

"Hey, is the building haunted?" He looked concerned.

"Not that I know of. Why?"

"The other night the curtains in the kitchen were blowing in and there was no wind. Then the lights flickered on and off ..."

"Might be a short. The wiring's old." Not that I knew what I was talking about.

He continued, not listening. "I was asleep and it felt like a pair of hands were trying to smother me."

Maybe he'd tapped into the collective unconscious of the tenants, who did all want to smother him.

"Maybe it's the pot making you paranoid."

"I wasn't even high. I yelled, 'Get off me' ... and it let go."

"Well. I did hear a woman jumped out the window in Judy's apartment years ago. The neighbors across the way heard her scream, 'The devil's escaped from hell,' and she did a header on the pavement."

"Then why doesn't she bother Judy?"

"Maybe she's scared of her."

"She's a bitch."

"Keep me posted if there's any more paranormal activity." I wondered which vendor I could tap for that one.

DATE	TRANSACTION DESCRIPTION	PAYMENT, FEE, WITHDRAWAL (-)	✓	DEPOSIT, CREDIT (+)	$
3.15.15	Unemployment (two weeks)			900.00	2,680.72
3.18.15	Vitamin C, floss	26.33			2,654.39
3.18.15	Hazelnut Cronut	1.41			2,652.98

7

The old Irishman—O'Mallory O'Shaunessey McGill from 205—was moving out to travel the country by RV, slipping the harness he'd been in while working at the local hardware store (his words). Other than the smell of boiled cabbage, potatoes and Guinness, he'd left his apartment in tip-top shape. O'Mallory O'Shaunessey McGill was a stand-up guy. Like all our conversations, O'Mallory O'Shaunessey McGill ended this one saying, "So it is." I never really understood what he meant by that. Was it a reference to Samuel Beckett? A James Joyce allusion? Flann O'Brien? It would remain a mystery.

There was a side benefit to the move-out inspection: a quartet of fine mahogany pieces that had eluded Brenda. O'Mallory O'Shaunessey McGill was ready to let them go. I coveted the slick pair of slim side-tables, perfect for nightstands, and the matching Art Deco lamps. I was getting on in years and wanted furniture that announced who I was. My id. The kidney-shaped chair anchored my space, was its focal point. I had that. And four new impact pieces, if negotiations went well.

In an effort to pre-empt any poaching by Brenda, I went in with a robust offer of $450; one week's full unemployment. It was an audacious, but I felt necessary, move on my part. O'Mallory O'Shaunessey McGill shook my hand and took the cash.

I was tempted to flaunt my newly acquired treasures. I could leave them outside my apartment, where Brenda would see them and stew about not getting her pilfering hands on them.

But karma could strike back, in unexpected, even deadly ways. Or Brenda would simply steal them when I was napping.

Once the id pieces were in my apartment, I stood visualizing gaps in the collection. I needed to manifest a desk, sofa and side banquette. I'd be patient, bide my time. There'd be turnover: deaths, evictions, and successful tenant-on-tenant violence. It would all work out.

Larry wanted Vasco to handle the renovations of O'Mallory O'Shaunessey McGill's unit, untouched since the great Irish potato famine. Or did that pre-date the building? I'd have to look it up. All I had to do was make sure Vasco and Cortez didn't conduct Santeria rituals during work hours and sign for deliveries.

The next hurdle was finding a new tenant with the appearance of mental stability, strong coping skills and no criminal record. I had my work cut out for me.

A "For Rent" sign, I was convinced, only drew in the underbelly of society. Craigslist was the way to go. "Huge One-Bedroom in Historic '20s Building" was my headline. Putting in buzzwords like French-windows, high ceilings and hardwood floors would set off a stampede of applicants. I'd wait for in-person interviews before mentioning the attempted murder, suicide and ghost.

I'd meet applicants dressed in business casual, clean-shaven and hair neatly groomed, subliminally conveying there were standards in this building. Wrinkled jeans and a T-shirt were fine for writing, but not during the critical tenant evaluation process.

I was, however, up in the air about whether to have a pen on me. Inevitably, someone would want to fill out an application on the spot, not have a pen, and want to use mine. I could lie and say I didn't have one, but I was a solid citizen. And I might need one. But with never-before-seen viruses crisscrossing the globe, a random applicant could transfer one via a shared pen, leading to the total collapse of my immune system at the hands of a new scourge. Washing my hands and face afterwards was no match for a burgeoning pandemic!

I settled on investing in a package of all-purpose Bic pens, handing them over without regret. I just needed to make sure there was absolutely no incidental physical contact. However, if an applicant carried a deadly air-borne virus, I was toast—pen or no pen. I could don a surgical mask, but that wouldn't convey the right impression.

The first people to show up were a girlfriend–boyfriend combo. The guy had beady eyes, which wasn't his fault, but wouldn't make contact with my non-beady eyes. He nodded approval when I mentioned the square footage. Choosing his words carefully, all he said was they needed more space. The girlfriend, looking tough like Rosie the Riveter, said nothing.

"Jeff," the name he used, inspected the garage that came with the unit, displaying an uncharacteristic attention to detail. What was he planning to put in there? Was it going to be a *Silence of the Lambs*–type storage scenario? Or was he checking the ventilation for a future meth lab? The real tip-off was when he asked what parking was like on the block. He told me they only had one car, worked from home, and weren't going to buy a second "ride."

"It's tight around the building." What were they up to? I tried to look into at least one of his beady eyes, with my nicely proportioned set of eyes, but it eluded me.

Was he being shifty, or was it just an optic condition?

Why all this concern about abundant parking? Jeff didn't mention an extended family or seem like the type to have fantasy football buddies dropping by. It was clear. They were drug dealers who within days would bring crime, prostitution and gambling into the area. This could be a boon to my writing. There was nothing like having material close at hand. But a sense of self-preservation got the best of me. I could wind up in the trunk of a car, like in the old neighborhood. They were out.

To cover my tracks with Jeff and his ilk, in the future I'd over-book appointments to dramatize interest in the place, so if I passed on anyone from the underbelly of society—like Jeff and Rosie the Riveter—I could say it went to one of the other many applicants, thus minimizing the risk of reprisals.

As they sped off to their current cook location, a chubby 30-something Armenian woman who went by Hasmid came over. She seemed nice enough.

Hasmid marveled at the ridiculous number of cabinets in the kitchen, trying to fathom what it all meant. Who built them, and why? Wanting to pick up the pace, I snapped her out of her trance, suggesting we check out the mountain views.

"They're French windows." I voiced one of my Craigslist buzzwords. Hasmid gave me a blank look. I guess the view was wasted on her when she was dreaming of stocking those cabinets high with canned chickpeas and boxes of kefir. "The apartment's just for you, right?"

"I have three children."

"Oh ... how old are they?"

"Three, five and nine."

"That's fine." It wasn't. I'd specifically asked her when we'd spoken over the phone if the place was just for her. She'd said yes, and now I had to wonder, if she'd already lied once, what was next? Hasmid's extended clan spanning three, four generations moving in? The butchering of live animals out back? Strip-mining?

Then again, it must have been difficult for mothers with children to find a rental. And they'd probably offer me slices of fresh meat, beautifully seasoned. Being both a compassionate and hungry person, I offered her an application.

I walked Hasmid outside, where we were met by an elderly Armenian couple.

"This is my parents. They live here too."

"Anyone else?"

She smiled. "My husband."

Brenda appeared in her window, sans Mikey, who was probably out banging stray cats. "Rupe. When's that dryer getting fixed?"

Her assumed familiarity irked me. "We're third on the list."

"I want to do my laundry."

"Understood. I'll keep you posted." No need to repeat the scenario of the one working dryer and Laundromat down the street. I'd be risking her and Marie teaming up, tracking my movements in and around the building, snipping the wires to the light sensors by the garages, using bird calls they'd practiced over and over again to communicate with one another, before stoning me under cover of darkness, my back turned while dumping trash in the bins.

As Brenda pulled back from her window, I turned to Hasmid. "Don't you think the place is a little small for ..." I ran a quick head count. "... seven people?"

"We fill out application. You talk to owner."

"Sure." I wondered if they were figuring out how to lay out the floor plan to include their cousins from the traveling Armenian circus: the fat woman, strong man—barbells in tow—and the tumbling midget troupe. I'd trash her application.

Men checked the water pressure. Women of all ages, races and creeds continued to marvel at the sheer number of kitchen cabinets. A hipster chick wearing a wife-beater, bra straps off to the side, brought a tape measure to challenge my square-footage figure. She lost. Otherwise, the mini-door outside the apartment piqued everyone's curiosity.

I took pleasure running down how in the days of the icebox—pre-refrigeration—the ice-man would deliver a block to each and every apartment. That bit of history resonated, sent people back in time. I added it to my spiel.

Next up, a dead-ringer for Charlie Chaplin in his *Limelight* days bounded up the stairs and slid into the place, arms splayed out. "I'll take it."

I liked him, despite the vaudeville jokes he hurled at me: "I'm on a roll, and I'm not even butter." Out of politeness, I didn't groan. Then I worried if his energy was masking severe depression. He could end up the second suicide in the building, ironically, in the same stack as the previous one. I was wavering on the guy, thinking about getting out the old vaudeville hook, when he asked if a piano would fit through the stairway doors. That would go over well. His banging out a series of oldies in our poorly insulated building would fire up the tenants to set on him with bricks, baseball bats and any other weapons they'd been harboring. And I'd get in a few good shots for the jokes he'd have been peppering me with.

"You can measure the doorways, but I doubt it."

"We can crane it through the windows."

"You want to pay for that?"

"Not me, the owner."

Next.

"Nice meeting you." I held out my hand.

A rogue's gallery of cretins, drunks and thieves followed: a guy and his stripper girlfriend—I wouldn't be having sex with her, so what was the point? Might as well bring back Jeff and Rosie for some excitement—sad sack stories of credit problems, people with "small dogs" that would turn out to be Neapolitan Mastiffs, Rottweilers and Doberman Pinschers capable of snapping me up like a cocktail-frank; the whale-sized teenager from the Inland Empire looking for her first apartment and fighting with her mother and smaller, baby-whale-sized sister as they checked it out, her footfalls destined to open fault lines that sucked the building, cars, trees, and a pile of complaint slips from Brenda to the bowels of the earth.

It was Monique who saved me. She was a winner. The minute I saw her approach the building with a broad smile and open face, I knew she was it. Put together, but still unassuming, you could tell right away she must have come from a good family. I couldn't find one fucked-up thing about her.

Before I even asked, Monique offered up that she was looking for herself and fiancé, LoKey. Was that really his name? I was intrigued. This could lead to Sunday morning brunches with Monique and LoKey, cracking open *The New York Times* magazine section, listening to Coltrane, discussing hair weaves in the African-American community and its social relevance while enjoying our multi-culti breakfast of bagels, lox and grits.

I was on pins and needles while we toured the apartment, waiting for Monique's response.

Please love it ... please want it ... please love it ...

"I love it."

She loved it. Now, I could focus and wonder where she'd put the large, well-worn Maasai-print armchair that I'd come to know as my own.

"What are the other tenants like?" I had to be honest, sort of. But did she really need to know all the gory details? I'd summarize.

"There's a strong sense of community. A few oddballs like everywhere. But it works." I opted to withhold my plan to save funds and put contracts out on a choice few. "When can I meet LoKey?" Hoping that didn't sound desperate.

"He's ten minutes out."

"Great." My voice cracked ever so slightly.

I had to make sure Larry would approve of Monique and LoKey. After he heard my adulation and encomiums for them and their high credit scores, he'd buy in hook, line and sinker.

Excitedly, I went ahead and prepared a lease, fished out a spare set of keys, and headed to the lobby with their nametag for the mailbox. So what if I was getting ahead of myself.

LoKey moving into the building was a coup for me. Other than our future Sunday morning rituals, I could count on him to know what the current brother handshakes were. I'd find the truth if the real brothers thought white guys routinely calling each other brother usurped its proprietary use in the black community. I'd wait for an opportunity to bring it up. Be natural about it, nonchalant. It was no big deal. We'd be close.

When I got to the lobby, Cortez was on his hands

and knees lifting up grime from the tiles. Vasco stood by, pointing out when Cortez missed a spot.

"Oh ... hi, Mr. Ru-pert ... I clean tile. Yes." "I" meaning Cortez was doing the cleaning while Vasco tallied his billable hours.

"Looks good."

"*Muy sucio.*"

Cortez grunted in agreement.

"Since you're here, can you start working on 302?"

"3-0-2?" Vasco puzzled over the complex sequence of numerals, as though I'd asked him a complicated theoretical physics question.

"The old guy."

Vasco took a moment to answer. He looked concerned. As if he was trying to figure out if Cortez had enough time to finish the entire lobby floor, go on another cerveza run to the bodega, and still fit in the carpet tacking.

"*Sábado.*"

I guess not.

A horrifying banshee wail flooded the hallways. Vasco and I looked at each other, bonding over our mutual fear. It got closer.

"You're ki—lllll—i—nnn—g meeee!" Marie cried, as she emerged from a side entrance, landing in a maelstrom of manic energy directed straight at Vasco.

Cortez made a stealth move for the door, looking for safer ground. I watched him jump into Vasco's truck, screeching off to the bodega ahead of schedule.

"Marie?" I stepped in to protect Vasco. I figured it was wiser to throw in with someone who could fix things, or someone who had someone to fix things.

"What's going on?" She turned toward me in slow motion, eyes blazing.

"You're using chemicals! You know I'm allergic to them." She pointed toward the puddles of solvent left by Cortez.

"We use 'organic." Vasco blurted out; he beamed with pride.

I was a bit surprised by Vasco's use of the term organic. It was usually associated with health food, and the last thing I'd seen him downing was a bag of hot Cheetos with Velveeta. Did he mean non-toxic? Were they equivalent? I reached for the bottle of solvent Cortez had dropped as he fled the premises, and saw inscribed across the front, in bold letters, non-toxic.

I presented Marie with the evidence. She was faltering upon cross-examination. But she wasn't gonna go down without a fight.

"It's his cologne!" She retorted.

I gave Vasco a good sniff myself, trying to get to the bottom of this crisis.

"It's beer. Cerveza." He said indignantly.

Fascinating! My Vasco–Cortez cerveza hypothesis was spot-on. As I pondered other problematic beverages, Monique and LoKey sauntered into our little domestic dysfunction.

I felt an inner panic. I couldn't afford any hiccups sealing the deal with Monique and LoKey.

It was like magic. All the tension in the lobby dialed right down as soon as they walked in with their mellow vibes. They were perfect.

Marie sniffed out Monique and LoKey. Unfazed, LoKey—who stood with a permanent lean, wearing a retro-Clyde-the-Glide Puma warm-up suit—extended his hand with total ease to Marie.

He must have smelled nice and clean to her. He did to me. She was happy. They shook. And after nodding politely toward Monique, Marie put on her best game face and turned to me. "My lock's sticking."

"We'll find an odor-free way to unstick it."

She eyed me, suspiciously, and sauntered off.

Monique and LoKey seemed nonplussed as Marie disappeared inside her lair, accompanied by the sound of a deadbolt, triple locks and a sliding door jam.

"She means well." I tried to sound convincing.

Hat Guy popped his head into the hallway. Could I not have a moment of peace to enjoy Monique and LoKey? "ETA on that dryer, Rupert?"

"Before you can change hats."

"Excellent." He removed his stingy brim, swept back a luxurious head of hair, and retreated into his compound.

At last. "LoKey ..." I said shying away from the familiar 'Key' form of address. "Can I show you the place?"

"Let's do the thing ..."

LoKey, a man of style, as evidenced by the aplomb with which he wore his throw-back Clyde-the-Glide warm-up suit, was into the place as much as Monique. I told them filling out the application was a formality; the place would be theirs if I had anything to say about it. I didn't want to tell them I'd already prepared a lease, set of keys, labeled their mailbox and planned our futures together.

I was on a natural high as I floated back upstairs.

Outside my apartment, I spotted Judy smoking on the balcony. She nodded to me.

Hmm ... interesting. Either A: She just took up

smoking. Today. B: She was always a smoker, but seems to think she should be the only one allowed to smoke in the building—an entitled smoker. Or C: She just used Jonas' smoking as an excuse to get me alone. I'm guessing its C. She's into me.

DATE	TRANSACTION DESCRIPTION	PAYMENT, FEE, WITHDRAWAL (-)	✓	DEPOSIT, CREDIT (+)	$
3.19.15	12-pack, Bic pens	3.61			2,649.37
3.31.15	"id" pieces of mahogany furniture	450.00			2,199.37

8

Now that the vacancy was filled to my satisfaction, I could shift gears and focus on the novel. No better place to begin with than the dedication page. But who to include? I didn't want to overlook anyone, potentially causing rifts or petty resentments. Then again, some people craved anonymity and would prefer to not be associated with the book. Those people would miss out on a chance at immortality.

Stick to family members? That would be my mother and father, deceased. What about my uncle Elwood? My mother's half-brother, he did a stretch at Joliet Correctional for fencing a truckload of stolen Jordache jeans before turning Jehovah's Witness. I didn't want to go down that rabbit hole. But would that indicate I had no one? Was that even true? No one visited me anymore, or called. It was like I'd been banished from my home planet, same as the Silver Surfer.

I could flip the movie credits scenario on its head and include a "No Thanks To" page. I'd start with Marie, and work my way back. They'd live on in infamy, forever branded with a modern-day Hester Prynne–like scarlet letter. Which letter? What about reprisals? Or ...

Hearing a commotion outside, I went to the window and saw a ladder arc upwards, boots scurrying toward the roof. Footsteps rumbled overhead. It was the fire department on one of their frequent training exercises. The Captain had told me the Dryden Arms presented unique challenges for a rescue, with our corner lot, raised rooftop wall, and front and rear fire escapes, and that's why they often chose to train here.

Excited, I went down to watch the show.

The Captain, unmistakable by the word "Captain" on his badge, nodded to me, acknowledging my authority at the property.

As the Captain spoke into his walkie-talkie—directing the action—the panel for the Dryden Arms version of *Hollywood Squares* took their positions. Brenda, Marie and Hat Guy leaned out their windows. Taking the host's role, I reminded them it was a training exercise, and debated grabbing the Captain's bullhorn to make sure they were listening. That's when I realized we were missing our center square, Paul Lynde. Thankfully, Jonas leapt through the front door.

"Hide the puppies." Jonas squealed. "Cruella DeVille is mad."

Jonas scampered off, and the supporting cast, reacting to the news of Judy's impending arrival, closed down the show. Marie slammed her window shut. She'd had enough. Hat Guy started in with a monologue on how the fire hose worked before feeling compelled to mention that there were bald spots on the lawn. The horrific sight of Brenda, who, cradling Mikey, asked the fire Captain if he liked her pussy, cut him off. I actually saw him break character and gag on that one.

Then Judy stormed onto the scene, menace in every step. She didn't take any changes in the building's Chi well. Judy whipped off her sunglasses and assessed the situation. Disdain was dripping from her brow. She approached me, and reflexively, I took a step backwards. "Watch and learn."

The Captain, a rare exception to the buff, *GQ*-looking firemen, had a bulbous nose, doughy face and receding hairline. He was in for it. She hit him like a backdraft.

Judy told the Captain she'd ruin his retirement plan. Destroy his 401k. That his children and their children would be in rubble. Their lineage over. None of them would become firemen, not even crossing guards. Would his fate have been less harsh had he been blessed with traditional fireman good looks?

Visibly shaken, and clearly wanting to call his nana, the Captain signaled to his team to wrap things up. Cruella was radiant, having enjoyed her first kill of the day. As if nothing had happened, she rejoined me.

"I have a splitting headache from this and a pile of manuscripts to get through. Everyone wants my opinion, my blessing, my approval. Being a lit agent isn't as glamorous as it ought to be."

Lit agent? I was stunned.

Judy patted me on the cheek. "Didn't you know?"

As Judy headed for the building, Hat Guy appeared out of nowhere, offering her a smoke. Did everyone but me know Judy smoked? She took a long drag, blew out a plume of smoke, and walked through the lobby. Now probably wasn't the right time to mention there was no smoking in the building's common areas. Hat Guy nodded to me, cigarette dangling from his lips, as he walked to one of his legally parked vans.

The millisecond I walked into the lobby, Brenda ambushed me. She was the building's private dick, knowing all movements of all things Dryden Arms. She acted as a human surveillance camera from behind her lacy curtains.

"That fucking Mexican is a thief." Brenda stood there indignantly, Mikey encased in her sausage arms. I could have sworn I caught Mikey giving me a smug look.

"He's not Mexican. He's Guatemalan."

"You know what I mean."

I didn't.

"He owes me money." Mikey got a freaky look in his eyes.

"Really? For what?"

"You know the storage area by the garages?"

"Right ..."

"So ... Mr. 'I no speaka English' ... he's so full of shit ... went in there ... what business he has in there ... I don't know..."

"I don't know either." Was there illegal cock-fighting going on? Besides the Santeria rituals? What business did *she* have in the building's storage area, anyway?

"I see him drive off with all these plastic tubs crammed in his truck ..." Brenda, sweating, let Mikey go. He started sprinting like a madman back and forth across the hallway in a demonstration of crazy power. "... filled with my special linens."

"Why do you have linens in there?"

"That's not the point. He took them. I told you, he's a thief."

Showing amazing stamina, Mikey hadn't let up on his wind sprints.

"I have to hear the Mexicans talking back there, shouting to one another ... why can't they park on the street?"

"They've got tools and materials to carry ..."

"It's like a construction zone back there. Vasco gets that buzz saw going in the workshop ... all that scraping and sanding ... what's he doing? ... its not worth it anymore."

Could this be the moment I'd been praying for? Where Brenda gave notice? I began imagining a life without her. How free would I be? Trips to the beach seemed within reach. I'd handle building-related issues with my toes dug into the warm California sand. Who knew, the cute Buddhist girl might come back into my life, offering sex as well as Buddhist instruction. The entire ethos, the very zeitgeist of the building would change. Peace would reign. Marie would find new meaning in her life, or be cruelly marginalized. We'd embrace in the hallways. Start a Thursday Night Happy Hour. Learn new and wonderful things about the world and each other.

Brenda pulled me back in.

"You need to see what he stole." Which seemed impossible, if it had been stolen. Wasn't it already gone? No sense quibbling with her.

After corralling Mikey, we headed for the garages. I'd wondered why Mikey didn't head for the hills when a tenant came through one of the outside doors. As an animal bearing heightened senses, Mikey must have been alerted to the terrible circumstances he was living under just by Brenda's grating tone of voice. Yet he stayed. Seeing them together in this way, I realized it was a case of Stockholm syndrome. He was her own little Patty Hearst, his mind twisted by her beliefs.

While we walked together, I observed some similarities in appearance between them. After all, they both had the same frizzy hairstyle—although Brenda's was red—and crazed look in their eyes; both had a low center of gravity, with Brenda topping off at no more than four-nine and a half. The main difference I could discern: Mikey was in tip-top physical condition, whereas Brenda rolled in at a deuce and a quarter—easy.

"Asshole Hat Guy blocked my garage this morning. Next time, he gets towed."

"Call me first, so he has a chance to move?"

"Are you kidding? I've logged his license plate. The next call goes to the tow company. I've got them on speed dial now."

"Uh ... okay."

Brenda fished a key out of her tent-sized Capri pants. She must have coaxed a bootleg copy out of the Magician by feeding his insatiable appetite for quarters. I let her go first, partially because I was a gentleman but mostly to allow her frizzed-out hair to catch any spider webs, clearing my path.

Brenda pulled a cord for the proverbial bare bulb that lit the spooky place. Amidst stacks of mismatched storage tubs and piles of broken furniture were porcelain figurines, teacup sets, lampshades, umbrella stands, lacy tablecloths—lace being a favorite material of Brenda's—wicker baskets, candlesticks, old framed photographs and silverware chests.

"What is all this stuff?"

"Mine."

"You opening a bed and breakfast?"

Ignoring me, Brenda dropped Mikey to the ground, where he proceeded to patrol the premises in an arrogant fashion, tail high, erect. Brenda pried open the lid of a dusty tub and presented a piece of fine linen for my inspection.

"The drunk Mexican missed THIS ONE."

So there was an un-stolen example of what had been stolen.

I was trying to pay attention to Brenda, but thought it prudent to keep an eye on the bulb to see if it A: sparked, or B: started swinging in the breezeless air—indicating paranormal activity. From the looks of things, this would be a prime hangout for Jonas's ghost. But hopefully she was confining herself to Jonas's apartment, targeting him in particular, on behalf of the current tenants. Not wanting to chance the ghost switching venues, locking us in and hurling supernatural forces at us, I led the way out.

Feeling safer in the light of day, I was better able to focus on Brenda's accusations about the drunken Mexican thief. Although, I could see Mikey was getting agitated by the threat of paranormal activity and the whiny pitch in Brenda's voice.

"What if I arranged for the safe return of the linens?"

Brenda clamped a hand down on my wrist. "Or cash compensation." A real sentimentalist.

"I'll do my best."

"And I'm withholding rent, if that dryer isn't fixed end of week."

"No need. Tomorrow's the day."

"So you say."

Brenda, now covered in a layer of grime mixed with sweat, scooped up Mikey, whose frizzy fur began to stick to her film. I had to avert my eyes. They trudged off.

To avoid awkward small talk with Brenda and Mikey, I lagged behind, checking to see if the first-floor back door—which you could exit, but not enter—was propped open with a rock. This was the Magician's unauthorized shortcut. He didn't want to walk all the way from his garage to the lobby entrance. I'd spied him in the act one time.

While I liked the guy, I had to put a stop to it. It was a security issue. Anyone could slip inside the building and wreak havoc; the tenants were under my protection.

I'd tried to address the problem by putting the rock back in the soil bed where the Magician had taken it. But then he'd go to the rock bed, take it, and prop the door back open. So we got into a vicious cycle of rock movements.

Finally, to put an end to the tedious cycle, I'd waited until the Magician drove off, loaded all the rocks in my car, and placed them in a crop circle formation on a stretch of Malibu beach.

My behavior modification program worked. The Magician capitulated or was too lazy to scout out new rocks. He began using the lobby door.

To make sure there weren't any lingering tensions over our silent rock war, I thought the two of us should spend some quality time together, go for a drive.

After two sharp raps on his door—cluing the Magician into my affinity for *The Postman Always Rings Twice*—he emerged from his magical realm in his usual garb of *SNL* T-shirt, shorts and flip-flops.

"What's up?"

Not detecting any anger, malice or tension from the rock situation in the Magician's voice, I went ahead with my offer.

"Want to take a drive?"

"I hardly know you." He was playing coy.

"Come on. To clear our heads."

"Give me five. I'll meet you outside."

When the Magician appeared at my car, I'd expected a change from his customary lightweight wear into something more temperature appropriate, but no, he'd merely applied a fresh coat of hair gel. He was ready to roll.

As we made our way eastbound in the

Mercedes—the last series manufactured and assembled in Germany and commonly referred to as a tank (the more people said that, the more tempted I was to test it out by plowing through carpet/vinyl guys' McMansions, demonic teenagers' skate parks and a certain bikram yoga studio, as an act of revenge for a groin pull)—a silver Porsche Panamera zoomed by. It was then that I realized how much I had in common with the Silver Surfer, as I did with Buk, maybe more. In fact, I had become the embodiment of the Silver Surfer, who, after saving the Earth, was confined to our solar system by Galactus, instead of roaming the galaxies as his herald. Granted, my confinement to Glendale and its immediate environs was self-imposed. But I always needed to be in striking distance should evil befall the building, or to make sure I was there in plenty of time to meet the termite inspector and others of his kind. Plus, I'd lost my patience with traffic tie-ups and was stricken by the lethargy caused from endless days of California sun—like so many others. So I was imprisoned like the Silver Surfer—minus the surfboard, superhero powers and sculpted physique.

Driving through Eagle Rock, I sensed an energy shift in the car. The Magician was growing agitated by the abundance of all-night donut shops we were passing. He drew on all his powers to withstand the temptation. I admired his strength and decided to seek his counsel.

"Why are the women in the building so angry? Whenever there's any kind of a problem, they act like I'd spit in their faces and called their mothers dirty whores. What's up with that?"

"It's a sickness. The ugliness on the inside shows on the outside. It's a manifestation of how they feel about themselves. They're in hell, one of the lowest worlds. Until they can feel better about themselves, they're gonna turn their anger outward at anyone that crosses their path, further repelling the world—and especially men. Sad, really."

Yes! I'd been overly critical of the tenants, generalizing, only seeing them at their worst moments. And focusing on the bad makeup, scent sensitivities, sausage arms ... Didn't Buddhism teach openness of mind? I wasn't their judge and jury. These were unhappy people, crying in the wilderness. I wasn't hearing them—until tonight!

"You're right."

"Not only that ... when the Magician says Santa Claus is coming to town, you better put up your stocking."

"That's funny."

"Of course it is. I said it. Listen, it's up to you Rupert. The only thing that can change in this situation is you. You need to change your thinking."

"I will. Hey, did you know Judy's a lit agent?"

"Then write your book and fuck her already."

It was so simple.

"And get that dryer fixed. You're not safe."

"Tomorrow. The repairman swore to me." The Magician must have been in a bind. Sacks of quarters he could only feed five at a time.

After our drive, I backed into my garage, the Magician waiting to lock it.

"I'll do it. Thanks, though."

"Goodnight, Rupert."

I watched him walk along the garages and disappear behind the building. I was intrigued that he went for the back door, the rocks having been long removed. I locked the garage, waited, and then followed.

He was gone. A large man, he didn't move that

quickly, especially in flip-flops.

The light over the back door spotlighted a Priority Mail package, propping it open. I took a few steps toward the box, bent down ... and stopped.

I stepped over it, and slipped inside the building, leaving it where it was.

DATE	TRANSACTION DESCRIPTION	PAYMENT, FEE, WITHDRAWAL (-)	✓	DEPOSIT, CREDIT (+)	$
4.2.15	Gas for Malibu and Eagle Rock trips	37.14			3,062.23

9

Sábado. Vasco was a no-show. Just as well, I didn't need the distraction. I dove back into the novel, wanting to keep up the momentum.

The dedication page well underway, I knew I had to start thinking through my acknowledgments; didn't want that to get away from me. I was hitting a wall when the *Mission Impossible* ringtone broke my steely concentration. It was Matt, the laundry repair guy. Not a moment too soon. The tenants had been on me like hyenas and vultures about the downed dryer.

I'd never had a particular interest in industrial laundry equipment, but Matt changed all that. He was powerful and weathered, like Robert Shaw's shark hunter in *Jaws.* I could tell this guy had seen some things that I never would.

"Tell me about the dryer," Matt asked in the basement.

"The machine started up ... then, when I came back downstairs ..."

"At the end of the cycle?"

"Yes."

"Go on."

"The clothes were damp."

"Damp like they'd been warmed? Or damp like the dryer never went on?"

"Warmed."

"What did do you then?"

Suddenly, it felt like I was being interrogated during the "Law" phase of the original *Law & Order*, not to be confused with *Special Victims Unit* or *Criminal Intent.*

"I put another five quarters in, and waited to see what would happen."

"What did happen?"

"About ten minutes into the drying cycle, the machine stopped."

"Did you open and close the dryer door and try to restart the machine?"

"I did."

"Did the cycle continue?"

"It did not."

Matt stood back, considering the possibilities, much as Shaw's Quint in *Jaws* did before his fateful, final shark-hunting voyage. Matt's eyes squinted. He breathed in deeply, filling his lungs. His eyes closed. I could feel his intensity grow, if that was even possible. I felt small.

"Now this is very important."

"I'm totally focused."

"After putting in the additional five quarters, did you stay with the clothes?"

"No. I headed back upstairs."

"So it is possible the machine could have turned back on."

"Possible, but not likely."

"Why do you say that?"

"The dampness of the clothes after the first and second failed attempts."

"Then it's the heating coil."

"Can you fix it?"

Matt gave me a look. Had I just offended him? You don't question Quint. However, if memory served, Quint did wind up getting eaten by the shark. Roy Scheider's sheriff had to save the day. And I was kind of a younger, better-looking version of Roy Scheider. I was ready and willing to attack the dryer, should Matt fall victim to this maintenance appointment.

He responded with a stoic confidence. "This is what I do."

My skills would not be needed this time around.

Back from his truck with a new heating coil, Matt took apart the lower panel of dryer #1. The repair well underway, Matt had the emotional space to mentor me.

"You know, Maytag invented the permanent press cycle in 1969."

"I didn't know that." Hat Guy probably knew it. I should have prepped better for this appointment.

"There's four minutes of no heat in the cycle, so the clothes can cool down ... like metal that's been bent and sets if it doesn't cool down. This way, wrinkles won't set when they're placed in the dryer."

"Ah, so the last four minutes is a preventive measure, keeping the clothes wrinkle-free ... eliminating the need for tiresome ironing and leaving more time for individual happiness."

"Exactly."

Matt patted my shoulder, a sparkle in his eye, as we headed up from the basement. I had done well. We were now bonded in what the Buddhists called the mentor–disciple relationship.

On the ground floor, repair done, Matt shared an interesting episode in the annals of washers and dryers: that Albert Einstein had actually tried to build a washing machine back in the '20s, but it kept catching fire or blowing up. I guess we all had to know our limits. But Einstein ultimately found his path.

"Why's it cost so much?" the Orc barked at us, rudely disrupting our civilized conversation. I did peek into his laundry basket, filled with risqué undergarments.

Irritated by the intrusion and flagrant disrespect, Matt fired back. "They're heavy-duty, industrial machines. Top of the line."

As far as I knew, there weren't any laundry machines in Middle-earth anyway. You just beat clothes against mossy rocks. The hobbits did their laundry that way.

"Relax." The Magician had slipped in through the Priority-Mail-package-propped-open back door. Feeling flush, he fished ten quarters out of a short pocket and sprinkled them into the Orc's laundry basket. He acknowledged the gift with a grunt, before charging down the basement steps.

The Magician nodded to me and Matt, then strode back into his magical realm.

My phone dinged with a text.

Marie: Update on the squeaky floor Rupert.

I texted back: *Sábado.* I mean Saturday.

Marie: I know Spanish.

End text bubble.

"Sorry about that."

"No need. You have your hands full here."

I felt understood, wished Matt could have hung

around all day sharing a bottle of wine and swapping stories. But Matt was in demand and had a schedule to keep. He said his farewells, as Hat Guy suddenly materialized like Nightcrawler in *X-2*.

"You need to see this." Hat Guy lit a cigarette—a law-abiding tenant—outside, as he led me to the lawn. It was his purview, from where he observed the comings and goings at the Dryden Arms. The self-proclaimed master of human behavior, ever vigilant, stood, a portrait in focus, overlooking his domain. If he was seeing something out of the ordinary, it was eluding me.

"What's up?"

"De Soto just left. He spent no more than thirty minutes—tops."

If Clint Eastwood ever decided to do a remake of *The Good, the Bad and the Ugly*, De Soto would be a slam-dunk to breathe new life into Eli Wallach's villainous Tuco. Only, De Soto was a whole lot taller and an actual Mexican, not a short Jew.

Topping off at six-six, he was a freak in his traditionally diminutive community. And with his missing teeth—the remaining stacked at crazy angles—half-shut eye and scarred face, he was fearsome to that community and to all the residents of the Dryden Arms. His leaf-blower was so big, even Maybelline's Orc would have had trouble maneuvering it. De Soto wielded it like a cheap, plastic toy. It was no wonder Hat Guy was complaining BEHIND his back.

"He's rushed. Our building's out of his way."

"See why we need a local crew for this?"

"It's not gonna happen. He's Duncan's guy."

"Have you seen Duncan Danforth's lawn?"

"Once."

"What did it look like?"

"Ever seen the Luxembourg Gardens?"

"Yeah. And we've got *Grey Gardens* over here, minus the cat feces." I didn't want to tell him that I'd recently spotted Mikey laying a turd behind the shrubs.

Hat Guy stubbed his cigarette out against the building's façade and stuck the butt in his jeans pocket. He closed his eyes, took a deep breath, sighed, and out it came.

"De Soto and his banditos just BLOW and go. You need to turn the soil. All they do is BLOW the stuff around ... BLOW it from one area to another ... they hardly pick up anything. I sweep all the dirt, debris and leaves to the curb ... put them in piles ... they literally have a fifth of a trashcan filled. A FIFTH! They should be filling that up every week ... they just BLOW the dirt into the street ... it gets pressed into the sidewalk, and STAINS it."

I was counting how many times Hat Guy used the word 'BLOW' when we locked eyes. Hat Guy had a wild look on his face.

"I understand." I didn't.

"All that shit comes right back up on the sidewalk. Whatever, dude. They're frickin' numbskulls. I do all this pre-work ..."

What the hell was pre-work? I wanted to know.

"... before the blow-and-goers come over ..."

As Hat Guy went on to detail the meaning of pre-work, I realized I was hungry. What should I have for lunch? If only there were a Wiener schnitzel truck in Glendale, like the one I'd heard about in New York that served authentic breaded veal cutlets. Out here, they only had the Wiener schnitzel fast-food chain that sold hot dogs; a clear perversion of Austria's national dish. Was it Germany's too? No, theirs was probably a bratwurst of some kind. Veal schnitzels had probably been banned, like foie gras. I was most likely looking at a chicken or pork version of the real thing, if the truck had even made it west. And what happened with the shark fin soup ban in San Francisco? Wasn't the Chinese-American community up in arms over that one? Sharks were a prehistoric predator with no place in today's oceans. Some other, more benign creature needed a turn at the top of the ocean food chain.

"... I'm spending twelve to fourteen hours on the lawn every week. I'm out here every day ... trimming this, doing that ... they won't do anything ..."

Wait ... wait ... wait. Were we still talking about the lawn?

"Was it just De Soto today?" Not that I cared that much, but it made me look like I was still paying attention.

"No ... he never shows up alone. All he does is let his banditos do whatever, while he's probably special-ordering a new variety of azaleas for the Danforth estate."

I did happen to know that De Soto was the most egregious offender of the "please don't block the driveway" dictum. I would have asked him to move, but by the look on his face, I was worried he'd spray me with a six-shooter. So he continued to remain dead center in the driveway.

Brenda, too stupid and racist to be afraid, left De Soto notes on his windshield threatening to have him towed. Either he couldn't read or didn't care. Nothing changed.

"Did you write the email?" I'd suggested Hat Guy put down his concerns and I'd forward them to Duncan Danforth. I wish they could cut me out of the loop, but Danforth liked to use me as a human shield between him and the tenants.

I figured an email from this model tenant might move Duncan Danforth to nudge De Soto in the right direction. Hat Guy was constantly improving the value of his apartment by buffing the parquet floors, replacing missing brass doorknobs and kitchen drawer pulls, installing period-correct light fixtures and more.

Hat Guy fished another cigarette out of his jeans pocket, bent over and, cupping his hands over the cigarette even though there wasn't the slightest breeze, lit it. "You don't know this about me, but I'm a great writer."

"Alright. Let me know when you have it." I tried to leave, but Hat Guy was quick. He crowded me, like some street thug in a B-movie, angled himself to cut off any escape routes back into the building, down the street, or across the lawn. I was trapped.

"There are certain things we have to make sure of about the soil underneath before we put in new turf ..."

Here we go again. This was Hat Guy's ultimate goal, his zero-sum game: rip out the hodge-podge of coral-like plants—so '80s he'd told me, the ineffective drip-system and all the plants and trees that were dying from De Soto's benign neglect. It wouldn't happen while Duncan Danforth was the owner.

"Ronnie asked ..." Ronnie was the home-and-garden Übermensch whom Hat Guy had brought over to consult with on all things lawn and botany in general. "'... How does it get water?' I told him it's a drip system. He wanted to know how old it is. They have it in artificial turf ... have to irrigate it from underneath ... have to replace it all the time."

My mind went blank. I tried telling myself, *You're curious, here's a chance to learn about home &*

gardening. I might have a house and garden one day and could use these tips. What if I found myself at a barbecue and the guys from the neighborhood association were facing similar lawn issues and I could weigh in, dazzling them with my erudition? But the longer Hat Guy went on, I felt myself slipping into a faint depression.

This saga had all started because of a single, ill-fated encounter between Hat Guy and Duncan Danforth, himself a gardening fanatic, who, oddly, visited the grounds of the Dryden Arms only once a season.

As Hat Guy had told it, Duncan Danforth showed up on his bike, complete with pedal-gripping shoes—preventing any wasted energy on the up-stroke—bike shorts, an aerodynamic helmet, gloves, you name it. Hat Guy had been appalled that this member of the landed gentry had presented himself in such an overly casual fashion. Did he think Duncan Danforth should be commuting in full foxhunt attire?

"You know what he did, Rupert?" Hat Guy had pounded on my door, desperate to tell his tale.

"Ah, actually I don't."

"I was shaping the hedges when Duncan Danforth meets up with De Soto for what I now have to assume was a pre-arranged meeting ... and they start surveying the lawn, taking measurements, soil samples ... what were they up to? I was standing right there. There was no acknowledgement, no eye contact. You'd think they'd want my input."

"I guess."

"I'm the one keeping the lawn alive!"

"It's a thankless job."

"They kept their distance from me, covering their mouths so I couldn't lip read."

"Like Joe Pesci in *Casino*, right? I love that

scene."

"The Feds didn't have the surveillance tools to crack that back then."

"Did you pick up anything?"

"Nah... they kept moving around. But I needed to know what the plan was. So I went up and extended my hand to Duncan Danforth. And you know what he said?"

"No, I wasn't there."

"He said, 'I'm the lawn Nazi.' Right off, that told me he didn't know Jewish history ... Finkelberger ... Finkel ... I'm a Sephardic Jew. Dude, no one knows what ethnicity I am." Which led to a dissertation on Jewish history and subsequent persecutions of the tribe. Interesting as the subject might have been—under different circumstances—the level of detail was crushing.

Exhaled cigarette smoke blowing across my face brought me back to the current—perceived—crisis.

"Even Vasco told me this morning ..."

What?! *Sábado*, and Vasco had been here? Then why hadn't he knocked on my door or let me know he was in the building? Was the appointment he'd set a ruse to keep me waiting—like a rube—inside my apartment while he stole the last of Brenda's special linens and checked to see if any clothes were left in the dryers that might fit him, his mother or Cortez? Vasco was bolder and soberer than I thought.

"...he moves so slowly, and you know what?"

"What?"

"...he says, 'What's the stuff all over your van?' It's resin, Rupert ..."

10

... *RESINA*! It's ruining my van. We need to cut down those trees ..." Hat Guy looked like his head was about to explode. I was worried because I'd heard Sephardic Jews had a propensity toward high blood pressure. "... which are nearly dead anyway, that's why they're shedding."

"Park somewhere else." It might save him from Brenda slashing his tires too. He ignored me.

"I shook the trees and all this stuff came down. It's getting in the plants; bugs like sugar-based things ..."

Hat Guy was stuck in an endless loop and he'd pulled me in with him. It was like being in Season 1, Episode 27 of the original *Star Trek*: "The Alternative Factor," where Lazarus traps himself inside a corridor between two universes with an anti-life other, sealed in ceaseless battle, so the other doesn't break through to Kirk's—and our—universe, destroying it.

"It's ruining the paint on my van, Rupert!" His face turned a deeper shade of crimson and he started to tear up.

Since I was horrified by the thought of having to give Hat Guy mouth-to-mouth if he passed out, I hatched an immediate plan.

"I'll call the city and see if they'll come out to trim the trees."

"They haven't done shit in two years." He panted. "I keep showing up at city council meetings, but can't even get on the agenda."

"Let me try."

"I don't know." He sighed, collected himself.

After a beat, he looked me dead in the eye. "That Eurasian chick Maybelline on the third-floor is a porn star." He was calming down.

"Really?" I grew excited, wondering if sex was in the offing. Not with Maybelline. She was taken, cordoned off from contact with other interested parties by the Orc. But one of her equally slutty friends, for whom sex didn't mean much, might be available. Probably not a relationship in the making, but who knew? One of them might be putting their porn money toward a Ph.D. in psychology. Then, I'd have the ideal woman—a porn star/psychotherapist–girlfriend. It could happen.

"Yeah ... I was relaxing ... watching my favorite adult channel last night ... and there she was ..."

"You sure?"

"Oh, yeah. I waited for the end credits to make a positive ID. Matched her face and screen name. Then I Googled her. She's got a HUGE repertoire. I'm gonna see 'em all. I'm turned on knowing she's right upstairs. Man, she's got a tight body."

"Did I ever tell you about those racks of clothes in her bedroom? And the boots?"

Hat Guy piled on. "AND the four-poster bed I helped her boyfriend drag up the stairs ..."

We both came to the same realization. "She's web-casting ..."

The Sephardic was starting to turn red again.

"Think she takes PayPal? Or offers a Dryden

Arms discount?"

"Bet she's making a killing."

With his signature move, Hat Guy stubbed his cigarette out against the façade and pocketed it. "Anyway, I've gotta go call Ronnie. He's been waiting." Like I'd been keeping HIM. At least my ordeal was over.

Back in my apartment, I knocked out a call to the Glendale Neighborhood Services department. Hat Guy was right. The city had suspended all tree trimming for the foreseeable future. Short of me, Hat Guy and Ronnie shimmying up the trees under cover of darkness—chainsaws in hand, ski masks on—there'd be no relief from the *resina*.

Settling back in the Aeron chair, I delved into the idea of writing a porn version of Buk's *Women*, inspired by Maybelline and co. It had all the elements: women and porn. This was in no way to be confused with Louisa May Alcott's *Little Women*. I didn't want the responsibility of traumatizing a bunch of fourth-grade schoolgirls and menopausal librarians.

I'd have to work my way up in the porn world. Start by getting coffee and lube. Chat up the actresses. They'd notice my boyish good looks. Make jokes about wanting to partner with me on camera, after I picked up their Vagisil. The Orc would take me under his wing. We'd take 'roids together, inject each other in the ass. I'd be one of them.

It was the next step that was daunting. I'd be offered a choice. Perform on camera, or lose access. Given that I suffered from moderate levels of anxiety—if a woman friend tried to hold hands in public—I knew I had a problem. Plus, I'd be forever recognizable—as a face and penis. Stopped in the street. Quizzical looks on faces, mostly from men. Unsure of where they knew me from. A growing sense of shame would force me into hiding, or to live abroad. What would I live off of?

A knock on the door interrupted my process. Not THE knock on the door, the cops finally catching up with me for a crime I committed ages ago. I hadn't committed any crimes, but the possibility always existed for some type of mistaken identity situation whereby I'd end up like Cary Grant in *North by Northwest*, forced to dig deep for mental resources I hadn't even known I possessed, unused tools in my already well-stocked mental toolkit, in order to escape the clutches of a nefarious organization hell-bent on stealing one or both of my kidneys for a dying despot in a far corner of the globe.

It was only Vasco. He didn't say anything about why he was just showing up now. Only that he was there to patch the hole in the wall. I'd gotten used to it. The hole had been there, pretty much, since I moved in. While Vasco got things rolling, I'd head out for a coffee, no, switch to green tea. Get my third-eye right.

But I couldn't leave Vasco alone in the apartment. If linens were his thing, I'd come back to find my bed stripped of my favorite Spider Man sheets, and my stolen hotel towels re-stolen.

I'd line the kitchen drawers with the starburst pattern I'd bought on eBay, a legitimate project, and keep a watchful eye on Vasco, leaving the bedroom door open—daring him to make a move on Spidey.

Between multiple measurings, repeated trips to the workshop to run the buzz saw and cut and re-cut plaster, it took Vasco the rest of the afternoon to patch the doggie door-sized hole.

I took my time lining the drawers, running scenarios about how to bring up Vasco's thievery. I had to be careful. I didn't want to wind up bound and gagged in the closet while Vasco made a run for the border, 800-

threadcount sheets in tow. As Vasco packed up, I worked up the nerve to confront him.

"I need to talk to you about something."

"It was accident. I didn't mean to walk in on naked lady."

"Which lady?"

"You know, sexy lady with ugly boyfriend."

"Maybelline? How'd that happen?"

"I knock on door. Check on patch in ceiling. No one answers. So I go in and see titties. I'm sorry, Mr. Rupert. She mad?"

"She never said a word."

"So what did you need to talk about, Mr. Rupert?"

"Brenda tells me you stole from her."

"I don't steal from the red pig, Mr. Rupert."

"She said you took her linens from the storage space."

Vasco shook his head in disbelief. "The red pig steal from those sick, old people when they die. She hides everything in there. It's no hers. She's the thief. I give to people who need. She just ... what's the word, Mr. Rupert? People who always keep things ... too many things ... only for self ..."

"A hoarder? Greedy?"

"*Es la verdad.* Is true. Yes. Si."

So ... let me get this straight. The red pig ... has picked over the bones of the weak and elderly ... is warehousing her stolen goods ... illegally ... on Dryden Arms premises ... without paying a storage fee ... and for a supply of quarters ... coerced a non-sanctioned key to said space. So basically I'm dealing with a compulsive liar, thief and potential criminal mastermind.

"If it's trouble for you, Mr. Rupert ... I bring back."

"No. I'm glad they're going to good use. And don't worry about the red pig. I'll take care of her." Vasco gave me a two-handed shake.

"Thank you, Mr. Rupert. I fix old man's carpet now."

DATE	TRANSACTION DESCRIPTION	PAYMENT, FEE, WITHDRAWAL (-)	✓	DEPOSIT, CREDIT (+)	$
4.4.15	Coffee, mini-cannoli	3.11			3,059.12
4.5.15	Tide detergent pods	5.69			3,053.43

11

I needed to unlock the floodgates of my mind. Let the dormant and repressed novel ideas flow freely. I'd bank on the concept that since we're 65% or so water, extended time with H_2O—in this case, under the shower—would be the key. Nothing flowed, so I took a bath figuring full body immersion would stimulate my mind. As the skin on my fingertips pruned, something else got stimulated. I had an erection. No ideas. I hadn't gone far enough.

The answer was TOTAL sensory deprivation. Like in that movie *Altered States* with William Hurt. By immersing himself in a floatation tank and taking psychoactive drugs, he was able to access previously inaccessible, primal parts of his brain that were no longer needed in modern-day society, but held the key to unadulterated creativity. I was determined to bring forth my prehistoric self, residing in the reptilian brain.

Since I didn't have a spirit guide for an acid trip and hallucinogenics were out of the question, I'd turn the bathroom into an isolation chamber creating my own version of a sensory deprivation tank. For total darkness, I draped a thick towel over the window. Now to float, I needed salt—lots of it. That giant, unused box of kosher salt I'd inherited, oddly enough, from O'Mallory O'Shaunessey McGill would finally come in handy. My face and body would skim the surface of the water, while my ears were submerged. All of my senses would be obscured. I'd have nothing to smell, touch, taste or see. My mind would roam free.

I eased myself into the temperature-neutral water and achieved a measure of buoyancy. Thank goodness for these deep, old tubs.

I was relaxing into it when the first images hit. I was a matzo ball floating around in a pot of soup. I could feel carrots, onions, chunks of celery and a wisp of dill brushing past me. I got hungry. I became a zeppole—one of my all-time favorite deep-fried pastries—crisping up in warm oil. Powdered sugar dusted me, like an early morning snow.

As my mouth opened to catch the sugar granules, the phone rang. I'd forgotten to turn off the ringer. I tried to ignore it by imagining the taste of the sugar on my tongue. The ringing persisted. I plunged myself back into the pot of soup, hoping the assorted vegetables and salt-saturated-water would buffer the sound of the phone. It didn't work.

Toweling off, erection back, I listened to the messages. It was Judy. She said she had an emergency in her apartment and needed to see me. I dressed and headed up.

"I hit my head in the shower ..."

Was I so powerful that I'd brought Judy and who knew what other tenants into a collective unconsciousness, centered on water and bathroom activities? Clearly, I needed to hear her experience.

"... I'm dizzy."

Had Judy taken the psychotropic route that I was too fearful of? It was time to compare results. "What happened?"

"There's an obstruction. I was seeing stars."

Wow. She actually had planetary activity. That

beat my matzo ball.

As we stood in her make-up strewn bathroom, I didn't see anything out of the ordinary. Judy kept pointing at the towel rack. I wondered what concept the towel rack represented to her. While I was pondering that question, Judy spoke up.

"I slipped and hit my head on the towel rack." I guess it actually represented the object that Judy hit her head on.

Shit! I'd have to take her to the ER. It meant hours waiting in a germy, airless room with pneumonia and bronchitis cases breathing all over me. And averting my eyes to a day's worth of Glendale's carnage: car accidents, a slip of a chainsaw or nail gun, tree-trimmers whose frayed ropes had finally given out. Maybe there was a close girlfriend or coworker that didn't despise Judy who'd step up and take her.

But then again, she was a lit agent and it would be a bonding opportunity. We'd have been through something together. I'd be her savior. She'd have to represent me.

I was still puzzling over how it happened. If Judy had in fact been taking a bath and stood up to get out, no matter how I pictured it, her head would have been above the towel rack. Standing and bending down for a bar of soap or loofah wouldn't have done it either. Judy was no Chinese acrobat with the flexibility to hit her head from that angle. The physics of it—Euclidean or quantum—just didn't work. It was a conundrum. Nonetheless, the last thing I needed on my hands was a subdural hematoma.

"I should take you to the emergency room."

"We'll now that you're here, I'm starting to feel a little better. Maybe you should sit with me for a little while and make sure I'm all right."

That was definitely a better use of my time.

"Okay."

Judy led me to a parlor-like sitting area. I noticed she'd hammered in Moroccan wall-mounted candleholders, which while setting a lovely mood, was a clear violation of her lease agreement. I'd let it slide, for now.

Judy pointed toward a rather grand, red leather quilted sofa. "Like it?"

"Sure."

"It's a Chesterfield.

"Like the cigarette?"

"That too. Come try it out."

I sat on the far end, away from Judy. She immediately slid close, rather quickly for someone with her type of injury. Upon closer examination, there was no physical evidence to back up Judy's story.

Judy rested her hand on my mid-thigh. The ER was definitely off the table.

The next thing I knew, that hand was rubbing my crotch and her tongue was halfway down my throat. Was I tasting a Cabernet? Hints of tangerine and a mixture of nuts hit me. Not only was she a smoker, but a day drinker too.

What to do? I wasn't really attracted to Judy, physically or emotionally. Plus, she was a tenant. And I was the manager. Was an un-crossable line now being crossed? Of course, if this were Maybelline, it would be completely fine.

Furthermore, I'd never been with a smoker. Secondhand smoke was a proven killer. Would I take up smoking? Shorten my lifespan. Stain my teeth and fingertips.

By this point, she'd unzipped me and was stroking my penis, getting me hard. I might have gone for it, had it not been for the constant texts dinging in my pocket.

I had to pry my mouth from Judy's to speak. "I'm so sorry. I have to look at this. It might be an emergency."

"Sure go ahead." Judy continued to stroke my penis.

Brenda was going berserk. Something had happened with LoKey.

"Oh, boy. This could be bad. I have to go deal with it."

"The Magician tells me you're some kind of great writer. When you come back for more, bring me your book. I'd love to look at it."

"I will. I'm tweaking it now." I guess there would be a next time.

Brenda, the serial texter, was waiting outside my apartment, pounding on the door. Glancing at her texts, I'd gleaned something about LoKey degrading the quality of life in the building. Brenda didn't paint a pretty picture this day, or any day. But today was particularly rough. Craning her neck out the window to spy on LoKey had exerted her too much. She was breathing hard and looked significantly clammier than usual.

"What's up?" I sounded stern. It was hard to muster love and compassion for the lying, stealing red pig.

"I don't want you to think I'm the nosy neighbor type ..."—which she was, and always would be—"... but we're no longer safe. It's LoKey. He's sitting out front ... legs spread apart ... acting like he owns the place ..."

"And?"

"Oh ... you know ... all proud ... his buddies hanging out in front of our building. Talking like they talk."

"Like how?"

"You know. All jive and funky handshakes."

Had I totally misread LoKey? Was Monique his high-priced woooommman that he'd acquired on his rise out of the hood, meant to throw me off the trail of his role in a widespread crack network? Would lower-level dealers stake their claim outside the Dryden Arms turning it into the Glendale, California version of *The Wire*'s infamous Franklin Terrace housing project? Bringing with them shuffling, muttering crack hoes in hoodies, flannels and big slippers, crying kids in tow, looking for their next score? Would I have to start donning Pumas, a silver do-rag and wield a 9-millimeter Glock just to get through the front door?

"Is he there now?"

"Uh huh ..."

"I have one quick thing to do. Then I'll head right down."

If LoKey was as much a threat to our way of life as Brenda was portraying, it was crucial, before the inevitable series of break-ins and robberies at gunpoint, that I hide my cufflink case, packed with vintage starburst links. Where would be safe? I settled on the bottom of the produce drawer, under the tangelos I got at Trader Joe's.

Reaching the lobby, I steeled myself to see LoKey sitting high up on the back of a discarded sofa on the front lawn, holding court and collecting rolls of cash, leaving marks in the soil that would torment Hat Guy, which I'd hear about in painstaking detail later.

But the reality wasn't nearly as colorful. LoKey was sitting on a bench in a J-Crew T-shirt and drawstring yoga pants chatting with another African-American friend in khakis and a polo shirt who seemed more like an accountant or paralegal than a deadly drug dealer. There was no hint of weapons, drugs or shuffling crack hoes. Only Monique—not hoed-up at all—stood out in Jackie O–style sunglasses and a casual, sporty Sunday look.

"Ready for brunch?" she said to the guys. And off they went, probably to the country club.

I nodded to them, realizing Brenda and Mikey were a far greater threat to my personal safety than LoKey and his accountant friend. What was the problem anyway? Was LoKey just too black for Brenda? How black was too black? Was Colin Powell the right kind of black? Tupac and Biggie were definitely way too black.

Approaching Brenda's lair to alleviate her racial concerns, I felt the staircase sway. Was it a tremor? No. It was Jonas, of course. He must have been wearing heavy boots and was shouting into his cell phone, which was a normal speaking voice for him. Jonas smiled, but waved me off with a shushing gesture. He may have been the loudest, least self-aware man alive. If I were him, I'd wear slippers and a bulletproof vest.

"See, Rupert." Brenda was braced inside her doorframe. Mikey sat erect in the hallway eager to hear what I had to say for myself, a smirk on his face. "What did I tell you? He's already bringing a bad element into the building." She was trying to muster me to her segregationist cause.

Yeah. LoKey's friend looked more like Steve Urkel from *Family Matters* than *The Wire*'s ruthless drug-lord Marlo Stanfield.

"I didn't see a problem."

"You know he acts blacker around his friends." She whispered. "The black ones."

"Huh?"

"Come on. You know. He gets all loud. Calls them 'Boyee.'" I almost laughed at her short, white, fat woman's impersonation of a black man.

"It's nothing to worry about. He's just having a good time."

Mikey was getting ticked off.

"By the way, what did the drunk Mexican say about my special linens?"

"He actually had another take on that. Like maybe they weren't yours to begin with."

"Oh, who cares anyway?"

I took that as her acquiescence.

"Come on, Mikey." He brushed past me and gave me a "fuck you" look.

I needed to chant to process this day. By bathing myself in a flood of positive cosmic energy, I'd put myself back on solid ground.

"Nam myo renge kyo ... Nam myo renge kyo ... Nam m ...."

Knock ... knock ... knock ... It was the Magician.

"Marie left her windows open."

"So?"

"We have to close them. She's out of town."

"There's NO WAY we can go in there."

"We have to. Someone can push the screens in and rob her."

Had he been talking to Brenda about LoKey and Steve Urkel? This was a tough one. The Magician had a point. On the other hand, Marie had beyond-strict rules about access to her space. There had been a trying negotiation about letting workmen in. There was a religious aura she didn't want disturbed. We'd settled on a protocol. Workers entered—shoes off—and were required to traverse Marie's homemade aluminum-foil version of the Yellow Brick Road. There'd be no veering off the path. I had to reassure the workers that I myself had survived being inside the belly of the beast, and that I wasn't sending them off to the alien mother ship for human probings. I guess we had to do it.

Moments later, we were outside Marie's digs, armed with a roll of Reynolds aluminum-foil. As I saw it, this was a two-man operation, although the Magician tried to send me in solo.

Because of my slimmer profile and agility, I was in the lead on hands and knees, shimmying along the slender foil path I was laying down in front of me. The Magician took up the rear, patting the foil firmly into place with his Fred Flintstone feet.

Suddenly, I was overcome with anxiety. I'd cheaped out and only bought the twenty-five-foot roll. I wasn't confident we'd make it all the way to the window before the foil ran out.

We'd made it halfway across the living room, when the mission blew up in our faces and the lights came on. Much to our mutual horror, Marie sat bolt upright in bed and screamed, "What the fuck!" She looked surprisingly like Marlon Brando in *Apocalypse Now*, except wearing a granny nightgown. She was almost as bald, displaying a few patches of uneven hair—kind of like an old poodle who'd been on the wrong side of a dogfight. It was a horrible image.

Through the abuses being hurled at us, we carefully tried to backtrack on the foil, each begging our version of forgiveness. On the dresser, a series of Styrofoam heads were decorated with Marie hair.

As we backed out the door the Magician shouted over me, in a pathetic attempt at small talk. "So, when ARE you going to New York?"

"NEXT WEEK!" Marie yelled back.

"Hey, by the way. That dryer's been fixed. It's working A-OKAY."

"GET THE FUCK OUT!"

Safely out in the hallway, I had to take stock of what had happened. The Magician and I had just been through something.

"Did you know?"

"Al—o—pecia." The Magician pronounced it like I was in kindergarten.

What came first? The meanness or the baldness? In any case, karma was a bitch, and so was Marie.

DATE	TRANSACTION DESCRIPTION	PAYMENT, FEE, WITHDRAWAL (-)	✓	DEPOSIT, CREDIT (+)	$
4.7.15	zeppole	2.68			1,112.74
4.7.15	Kosher salt	1.24			1,111.50

12

Needing space to absorb the Judy thing, I headed for the coffee shop. It was my version of *Cheers*. A place to get away, leave my troubles behind, where they're glad I came ...

Heavyset—my archenemy, by association with Don—was behind the counter, almost daring me to order something. We eyed each other as if in the climactic scene from *The Good, the Bad and the Ugly*. Heavyset was "The Bad"—but sported more facial hair than Lee Van Cleef. Tuco, a.k.a. De Soto ("The Ugly"), was probably pruning the rose bushes at Duncan Danforth's estate and couldn't be with us today, leaving me (like Clint Eastwood, "The Good") to deal with matters on my own.

Not trusting the shifty look in Heavyset's eyes, I opted for self-preservation and went with tea. A sealed tea bag in plain hot water was a safer move than her dosing me with God knows what coffee concoction.

Heavyset huffed, fluttering the hairs on her 'stache, irritated at having to pour hot water in a cup. She practically threw the tea bag at me, like a Chinese ninja star. Needless to say, I snubbed the tip jar, even though I was flush with change. There'd been no recent quarter shakedowns by the Magician.

In an attempt to irritate Heavyset with my mere presence, I delayed my departure, tearing open the tea bag and going through a prolonged steeping process right at the register. But the tremors from Heavyset's footsteps as she lumbered behind the counter got on my nerves and started to give me a headache.

All right, this wasn't *Cheers.* And Heavyset certainly didn't know my name.

I took it outside. Sat at a table sipping my tea. A group of older Armenian men were across from me, sitting under an umbrella smoking cigars and drinking their native brew from demitasse cups. What they didn't know was that my heavily steeped Earl Grey could go head-to-head with their mud-thick Armenian brew.

As the tea warmed me internally and the winter sun externally, I took stock. Had I hit the lottery with Judy? I'd get blown on a regular basis, have top-notch literary representation, snag a primo publishing deal, the best stylist for the jacket cover and be free to write days, bang Judy nights, and rough her up when the mood struck me. Like all the great writers. And dump her once I became successful.

Of course if it did go badly, there'd be factions in the building debating who was to blame. All I needed was Judy to rally Marie and Brenda to shiv me in the laundry room, despite having repaired the dryer. The best I could do was gather Don and the Magician to my side. And if I could get Hat Guy to shift his focus from the lawn, he might throw in on my behalf.

Maybe I was being shortsighted. But I wasn't feeling it. Attraction is an intangible thing. Or, the fact that Judy was a self-centered, mean-spirited, unattractive smoker played into it. The Magician wouldn't be happy with me.

Another pressing matter needed tending to. Since I didn't know if, in a bit of revisionist history, the Magician had pinned the whole break-in—as Marie had begun calling it—on me, I took action to exonerate myself. This time, rather than simply leaving Marie's paper outside her front door, I'd go to the trouble of removing it from its sprinkler-soaked plastic bag, presenting her with an air-dried, pristine periodical. Surely even someone as self-involved as Marie would notice the consideration I was extending to her and not demand to have me fired. After all, I'd used up an entire twenty-five-foot roll of aluminum foil.

Returning from the *Cheer*-less coffee shop, the moment I reached for Marie's paper, Hat Guy was on me. He could have been lying in wait, since I knew he monitored my movements in and around the building. On the other hand, was he a human seismograph, skilled at knowing the exact patterning, weight and velocity of footsteps, cueing him to my presence this morning?

"They laid down mulch!" Hat Guy was frantic, his face beet red.

"What?" Why couldn't I just pick up Marie's paper in peace?

Oblivious to my indifference and inexplicably freaked out by this latest affront to botany, Hat Guy launched into it.

"Look at this!"

The mounds of sea-spore grass and towering plants that dotted the front lawn had been blanketed with mulch.

"Okay. So, what's the problem?"

He visibly twitched. "Dude! The ground cover has BUGS in it. Do you know what's going to happen? Do you know what it's gonna do?"

"No."

"Man ... this is treated wood. Blocks of wood, broom handles ... you need to irrigate this so it doesn't get moldy. Your soil is turning into SAND! All the little shade palms are dying. The water has nowhere to go. It's sitting up top. The sun burns them ... the green plants will survive, the yellow ones will be eaten up by bugs, the shade plants will be dead ... they waited until I was out of town to do it. I knew I shouldn't have left."

Hat Guy was panting and snorting like an overweight pug.

"They've probably been watching you." Feeding his paranoia.

"Of course. De Soto knows I watch him. He's a rat. I bet he called Duncan Danforth to tell him the coast was clear."

Somehow, I doubted Duncan Danforth was sitting around on his estate waiting for the high-sign from De Soto that the midnight mulching operation was on.

"My friend Ronnie came by ... he lives out in the Bakersfield area ... he's doing a schoolyard out here in La Cañada using fake grass ... EasyTurf ... for insurance purposes ... kids can get infections ... whatever ..."

What this had to do with anything was beyond me. I decided to throw gas on the fire. "How're the bushes doing along the main driveway?"

"I don't even know what to tell you about that, those branches are so brittle and dry, I don't know whether that's an irrigation issue or ..." He pointed back at the mulch. "This isn't ground cover. There's ground cover for open areas. For plants you use bark or rocks ... bark! Water will go in between ... this is only soaking it up."

Hat Guy was wild.

"This is coming from Ronnie. A SPECIALIST." Hat Guy looked me dead in the eye. "Who does this for a damn living. He's the real deal ... he's my buddy, we talk all the time, he's teaching me how to smoke meat, bratwurst ... dammit ... that is not the right ground cover ..."

He kicked a clod of soil.

Bratwurst?

"Look at this. It's too dry ... you've got to get in here with a trowel and break up the soil ... bushes will survive, they're arid bushes ..."

I needed to know more about this Ronnie dude. I love smoked meats.

"So when's Ronnie coming by?" Planning out my next meal.

"Not soon enough ... last time he was over here we hung out ... he came in for an A&W root beer and we were just kicking the shit ... he thought the front ones looked okay ... the little ones I manicured ... they belong to the Japanese family ... rock huggers ... they're meant to go up against rock and be trimmed ... earth and ore together—a Zen kind of thing ..."

With shaky fingers, Hat Guy pulled a cigarette from a pack in his jeans pocket. He snapped it in two.

"We need Ronnie." I egged him on.

"I know, dude. The acacia trees are half-dead already. You NEED to get in touch with Duncan Danforth and get this taken care of. It's gonna be a hot summer. You have to fertilize the soil every year or two ... there's one hundred-plus plants. It is not low maintenance!"

Was Hat Guy gay? God knows he had a huge hard-on for Ronnie, with his smoked meats and mad gardening skills. Was this fanaticism all a ruse, a cover to spend time with Ronnie and me, establishing a rapport over what *some* would think of as a feminine subject? Just a thought.

"... that German chick who moved in ..."

Perhaps reading that I might be on to him, Hat Guy switched things up.

"Astrid?"

"five-five, medium-blonde, wears powder-blue track suits ..."

"Yeah?"

"She's got a roommate now."

"No, she doesn't."

"Yes, she does. I was trained by the FBI to notice these things."

Hmm. Had Hat Guy been one of those early nursery school recruits who'd demonstrated an uncanny prowess with block-building and a need to spy on other kids during naptime? "So you were in the actual FBI?"

"Yeah. My high school guidance counselor recommended me to the Bureau for testing. Highest score they'd seen in twenty years. They put me through college ... started training me. But I decided to do my own thing ... I really dig the whole mid-century modern movement ..."

I cut him off. "Anyway, Astrid doesn't have a roommate."

"Taller blonde, nice highlights, business-type ... always clutching a briefcase in her hand ... tight."

"It's Astrid in high heels and work clothes."

"They're two different people. Dude, I know what Astrid looks like, and that isn't her." He sniggered.

"Look, even if she does have a roommate ..."

"... not 'if.'"

"Whatever ... I haven't had any complaints about this phantom roommate ..."

Hat Guy gave me an irritated look. "I'm telling you, there's someone else living in that apartment ... Dude, I wish I had time to discuss this with you all morning, but I've gotta go take a piss and text Ronnie."

I finally dropped off Marie's paper—all but ironed for her like I was her own personal valet—and touched my big toe down on the second-floor landing, when Jonas came at me.

"So ... what's up with 'naked man'?"

"Naked what?"

"Old guy."

Wow. Don was running with that whole nudist thing, taking it into the building's common areas. Way to go old man. Don had more guts than I did.

"Was he fully naked?" Please say no.

"Pretty damn close. He had some fucking dishrag wrapped around him. Old flesh doesn't really do it for me."

"I'll work something out." Did that fall under my job description, keeping the elderly from inadvertently flashing the Dryden Arms community?

"And how come those laundry lines are still up? Didn't we get cited for that?"

"Yeah ... I know ... they need to come down ... I just feel bad. The old man likes to air-dry his clothes old school."

But I had to do it. Next time the inspector came out, we'd be fined.

"Cut 'em down man. Old guy will have to dry his dish rags like the rest of us."

Jonas was right. I'd cut them down today.

Wanting to do right by Don, I had an idea that would take the sting out of losing the laundry lines. I remembered seeing an old accordion-style drying rack amongst Brenda's stolen goods in the storage area. I went to investigate.

Sure enough, I found it on the top-shelf. Not easily, as it was wedged between two large plastic bins. This would do the trick for Don. Lifting it down, I spotted my long-missing, favorite desk blotter and letter opener, which I'd assumed got lost in the move. That red pig bitch must have stolen it from me on moving day. I took a quick inventory to see what else sticky fingers made off with. And wouldn't you know it, I found my Yosemite Sam salt and pepper shakers. Given the opportunity, I bet she'd drill the silver fillings out of my cavities as I slept.

Clothes rack in hand, I knocked on Don's door and prepared myself for an extended wait, as usual. Much to my surprise, I barely had time to get through two bars of the *Jeopardy* theme song, when Don appeared—fully clothed.

"I have some disappointing news ..."

"Oh ...

"The laundry lines have to come down. Insurance reasons."

Don looked somber as he took it in. What would this mean for his laundering future?

"But ... here's the good news." I gave a game-show hostess flourish. "... you can have this ..."—I showed him the clothes rack—"... and leave your windows open."

"That looks expensive."

It wasn't. But Don was still worried about money.

"It's a gift from the building."

Don seemed relieved. "Thank you. Would you mind if I asked you to help me with something?"

"Sure, Don."

"I've been trying to find these old movies and whenever I go to the video store, they say I need to check that Internet. Do you have a way to check the Internet?"

I couldn't help but smile. "I do."

"Well ... I have a list of ..." He pronounced it with gravitas "... film noir ... pictures I haven't seen in years ... Do you know what those are?"

Of course I did. But I decided to give him a chance to teach me about something he knew well. "Sort of. Actually, I know a great video store that has those kinds of movies. I can take you there, and you can tell me about film noir."

"I can pay for gas."

"Not necessary. I get thirty miles per gallon, city."

"I haven't been in an automobile for quite some time."

"Let me know when you want to go."

"I will ... I will." Don looked excited, but a little nervous at the magnitude of this venture. I'd let him wrap his head around it, and get back to me.

Perched on a rickety ladder, working a pair of pruning shears into a laundry line, I wondered why I had such a connection with Don. It was more than the film noir connection and love of baked goods. Now that I thought about it, I realized how much I had in common with the elderly, on a global level.

We were solitary creatures; reserved, polite, decent. Dipping into physical decline, Don handled it with grace. No complaints. Much the way I accepted diminished hearing, pops in my right knee and a lack of mental focus.

Don and I went about our business with aplomb. We were self-sufficient, self-sustaining beings. I was on track to end up alone too—unless the Judy situation panned out better than expected. Perhaps I'd cross paths with a Gen Z who'd bring me knowledge of the technological marvels bound to crop up in the coming decades.

What would I share with my younger protégé? Anecdotes? A short menu of stories from my past? No. I needed a specialty to keep their interest. I had none. That would prove problematic. Or, I could go on JDate and get married ...

"Yo, Rupert. How ya doin'?" LoKey hit me with his late-night DJ voice.

"Yo, Key." I threw back at him, sounding like an excited six-year-old girl gleefully atop the ladder. I hoped I hadn't overstepped by addressing him with the more familiar form of his name.

The flicker of a smile crossed his face. I guess I was good.

"Hey, any word on that garage opener?"

Dammit! I'd totally let the Key down. LoKey had asked for an automatic garage door opener a few weeks back, and when I ran into an insurmountable obstacle, I'd dropped the ball.

"Oh, man. I'm sorry. There's a hitch. Turns out Vasco can run power from the workshop, but it has to go through all the garages, and Brenda said hers is off-limits."

"What's it to her?"

"She's a bitch."

"I do anything to her?"

I wanted to tell him, *Yeah, as a matter of fact, you're black*. But felt that might make the Dryden Arms a race riot flash point.

"No. That's how she is. I can get Duncan Danforth involved."

"Nah ... I don't want to make a thing about it."

"You sure?"

"Yeah ... it's all cool man ..."

A lesser man would have gone after the red pig. But LoKey was in fact low-key. I felt safe to talk to him about one of my long-repressed concerns.

"Key?" I was still a little nervous.

He eyed me, like he knew what was coming: a request for information held tight and rarely, if ever, revealed outside the black community. What did I have to offer him in exchange? The secret to a fluffy matzo ball? Would that be enough? We'd see.

Slowly, I climbed down from the ladder, putting us on equal footing. I went in.

"I need to ask you something, if you don't mind."

"Go."

"Okay. Is this how the brothers shake?" I grabbed his hand in a wrestling grip and pulled him toward me, for the classic half-hug move. Key pressed against me, a curious look on his face.

"My personal preference is the straight shake. Some brothers are into the half-hug. To each his own."

Fascinating! I felt empowered enough to roll into part two.

"So ... does it bother the brothers, when we white guys say 'brother'?"

"Nah ... it's cool." What a relief. I was at last sociologically satisfied.

As LoKey sauntered off, I shouted down the

driveway after him. "Hey, Key. One more thing." Again, sounding like a six-year-old girl. "What does it mean when brothers say 'bra'?"

"Old school, Rupe." He had to laugh.

It had been a very full day. I needed some relaxation. An extended tug was in order. This time, the two black-haired Irish beauties returned. It started with them washing down their family's black stallion with a soapy bucket of water, and then they inadvertently got all soapy and naked themselves. I was pulled into a barnyard shower scene, in which I replaced the stallion as the focus of their attentions. I tried working Judy into the picture. She was wearing a tightly corseted, shiny black leather dominatrix getup—whip in hand. As she dropped to her knees to blow me, it was a buzzkill. And the black-haired Irish beauties split.

Lying in bed frustrated that Judy had spoiled my night, I rallied. Moved on to grapple with the problem of naming the protagonist in my impending novel. How had LoKey come up with his name? Was it given to him at birth, in the hospital? Were his parents that cool? Or was his birth-name actually Irwin, and by high school he was done with it? Irwin was long gone by the time LoKey met Monique. It was a mystery. More questions for Mr. Key to answer.

What about Buk? He went with Henry Chinaski. Chinaski, Bukowski. Not much of a disguise there. I wondered why Buk had felt the need to create a nom de guerre? Was it about distancing himself from the source material? Literary space? There was no mention of why in the letters or biographies. Well ... if Buk did it, I'd raise myself up on the giant's shoulders and do the same. But it was too soon. Without knowing what I'd write about, I'd remain nameless until further notice. The unnamable ... unknowable ... "zzz ..."

DATE	TRANSACTION DESCRIPTION	PAYMENT, FEE, WITHDRAWAL (-)	✓	DEPOSIT, CREDIT (+)	$
4.8.15	Tea, Cruffin	3.54			1,107.96
4.11.15	Fifty-foot roll of Reynolds Wrap	14.00			1,093.96

13

The time was right to start putting some serious thought into my picture for the novel's dust jacket. Buk was no help here. He was much older and unattractive by the time he was posing for dust jackets. Although there was a beauty to his full-face, eyes-shut-in-inner-contemplation, acne vulgaris shot on the cover of *Erections, Ejaculations, Exhibitions and General Tales of Ordinary Madness.* Actually, my looks weren't rough enough. I might not be taken seriously, written off as some boy-toy celebrity.

I'd need to explore weightier options: loop-collar rockabilly, Frank Sinatra gangster-crooner, retro-pimp, Jimi Hendrix Hussars jacket period. Or I could go with a disheveled, angry Norman Mailer vibe. I bet Judy would opt for the tweed jacket and crisp white shirt, unbuttoned at the top.

It'd be a big decision how I presented myself to the world. Warm, friendly guy next door. Angry depressive. Solemn, yet clever. Populist. Portland coffee house–type. There should be a certain intensity in my eyes, regardless. What about an Oscar Wilde flamboyance? Thank God I was putting my attention to this now. It would prove to be an enormous undertaking and a huge mistake to leave it to the last minute.

Exhausted from the morning's mental work, I went to fill my lungs with fresh air.

On the ground floor, I was puzzled to see the

back door closed. I went to investigate.

From the outside, it was locked. There wasn't a Priority Mail package, stones, or any other wedgeable objects in sight. Curious. Had the Magician voluntarily gone straight? Considered the risk he'd been posing to the other tenants?

Just then the Magician's door flew open and, looking worried, he pulled me into his magical realm. Which on closer inspection turned out to be not quite that magical. There was an empty card table, a bookcase crammed with trick reference manuals and a foldout couch. I was disappointed there was no sawing-a-woman-in-two box, nose-twitching rabbits or top hat and white gloves. Only a giant tub of hair gel on the kitchen counter.

"Mikey's missing." He blurted out.

"What?"

"Brenda's been looking for him."

"He probably got bored and went out to terrorize the neighborhood."

"What if something happens to him? I'd feel responsible."

We gave each other a knowing look. "That little white furry fucker was strong enough to push open the back door!"

"Then he WANTED to get out. So it's not on me, right?"

"Of course not."

"Should we help Brenda look?"

"Nah. I'm sure he'll come back when he's good and ready. Mikey walks to his own drummer."

"Yeah ... yeah. Okay ... he'll be fine."

Next order of business was Marie's paper.

I was on autopilot heading out to grab it, when I ran into Hat Guy. You would think by now that I'd have timed my mornings more prudently to avoid the never-ending loop of lawn dialogue.

But there he was, performing unauthorized lawn care. He was on his knees, head tucked like a swan, trimming the crab grass. Sensing my presence, he swiveled his head in my direction, and with a telltale Hat Guy gesture, removed his fedora, swept back his hair, and replaced what was, I admit, a fetching hat.

"Hey, Rupert ..."

"Nice hat." It was a calculated move to steer the conversation off the lawn.

"It's a trilby fedora. Worn just above the ears."

"I like it. It's cool, man."

"You can't get a hat like this today. They banned the chemicals used to get the finish."

"So where'd you get that one?"

"It's not easy. Hard to find. I have to network, man. Feel the finish."

Hat Guy extended the fedora and as I strode toward him, I felt my left ankle turn, lunged forward, and landed with a dull thud on a paving stone by the rose bushes. Searing pain shot through my left kneecap. The twisted and probably sprained ankle was negligible in comparison. I curled up in the fetal position, clutching my knee, nauseated.

"This lawn is a menace ..." Hat Guy raged. And mirroring Scarlett O'Hara wielding her clenched fist, declaring, "As God is my witness, I'll never be hungry again," Hat Guy—as passionately—raised a clump of crab grass to the sky and slammed it to the Earth, and as God was his witness—this crab grass ... had ... to ... go! No one would ever fall again. I could almost hear the orchestral music swelling, as I noticed a slight glistening in Hat Guy's eyes—perhaps a tear.

"That's the one you tripped over ... I saw it ... dude ... you flew across the lawn ..."

"I hope I didn't break anything."

"It's a bone bruise."

Hat Guy helped me to my feet and, wrapping an arm around my waist, led me, injured leg dragging across our version of a battlefield, to one of the stone benches.

"You have to talk to Duncan Danforth. You're the fourth or fifth person who's taken a dive on this lawn from hell. You should have seen when the mail carrier went down on this killing field. It was like a scene out of 'Nam. She rolled on her side, got up, and shook it right off. Had to be ex-military. Danforth is gonna have to put in a proper lawn."

"I doubt it."

"Ronnie's explained the liability issues to me."

"You don't have to worry about it. You're not the owner, only a concerned citizen."

"I followed her."

"Who?"

"Astrid's roommate. You know, 203."

"You saw them together?"

"No. Just the roommate. Come on, track with me dude. That fall must have really messed you up."

The only explanations I could come up with were A: Mystique from the *X-Men* had moved in. Not likely. Or B: the ghost Jonas saw was on the move. But wouldn't that make her Jonas's roommate, technically speaking? I asked Hat Guy pointedly. "Any chance the roommate could have been an apparition dressed in business casual? Because I might have a lead."

"What are you talking about?"

"There's a ghost in the building."

"We all know it's haunted. And P.S.: ghosts don't have that kind of gait."

"How do you know what kind of gait ghosts have? It's not all chain dragging."

Hat Guy shook his head at me, as if I were too much of a simpleton.

"Let's just settle this." I dialed Astrid's number.

"Put it on speaker. And don't let her off the hook until she fesses up." Hat Guy had a smug look on his face, anticipating certain victory.

"I'll do the talking."

Hat Guy arched an eyebrow and crowded me. He smelled of freshly clipped grass and fertilizer.

Astrid picked up and I laid it out for her, minus the ghost. She heard me out, and earnestly replied. "I would never do that without permission. And I have no desire to have a roommate. Can I ask what gave you that idea?"

"Well ... one of the tenants raised a concern."

"You mean the guy with the hat who's been following me?"

I glared at Hat Guy. Clearly, his espionage skills weren't all they were cracked up to be.

"I can't believe she spotted the tail," Hat Guy muttered under his breath, looking upset with himself.

"Yeah. He's made building security a personal hobby, ever since the shooting. He's harmless."

"It's making me uncomfortable."

"Don't blame you. I'll tell him to tail someone else."

"Good."

I tapped off and gave Hat Guy a look. "I told you there's no roommate."

"I'm confused. Hang tight. I'm gonna get to the bottom of this." He stormed back into the building, probably dusting for prints on his way and preparing to launch a massive Google search.

Scooping up Marie's paper, I went inside and found a pair of black children sharing a chair and playing Bakugan. Not knowing their names, I tracked them based on their eyewear or lack thereof.

"Did you see me fall?"

"Yeah, that looked bad," Glasses said.

"You live here?" No-Glasses asked.

"I'm Rupert, the manager."

"Cool. Then you know our dad. LoKey." No-Glasses said.

"I wish I had a cool name like your dad's."

"Yeah, Ru—p—ert." Glasses giggled.

"Hey, I didn't pick it. They gave me some dead uncle's name. What are your names?"

"DeAndre," Glasses said.

"Lamar," his brother a.k.a. No-Glasses said.

"Nice to meet you guys. Give me a sec." I propped Marie's paper against her door and continued talking to the boys.

"Either one of you know who the Silver Surfer is?"

"No. Why?" DeAndre asked.

"He's the best thing ever. I totally identify with him. He stood up to Galactus and got banned to our Solar Syst ..."

"What ... is ... this ... doing here?" Marie had thrown her door open, grabbed the paper, and was waving it in my face.

"I thought you wanted it brought in."

"Not so everyone can see it. Are you trying to embarrass me?"

"Why would I do that?"

"You tell me."

"I'm not sure what's happening here."

"Are you really that naïve?"

"About?"

"Put it here!" She pointed to the unused mini-ice door. "So no one can see it."

"But they still can."

"Not when they walk in the door."

"What does it matter?"

"I want it there!" She slammed her door shut.

I turned back to the kids.

"You in trouble, Rupert?" Lamar asked.

"You gonna be like that Silver Surfer man and get banned by that bad lady?" DeAndre wondered.

"Nah. She can't ban me. Anyway, the Silver Surfer fears nothing."

"Cool," DeAndre said.

"What do you two make of that whole thing?"

"That mean lady just feels stupid. She doesn't want the other people to know you do her work for her ... making you get her paper," Lamar explained.

"You think?"

"Her leg's not broken. My mama would make me get my own," Lamar continued.

"Well ... you've got a good mother. Thanks for clarifying that, guys."

"No problem, Rupert." Lamar said. They went back to their video game.

I staggered up the stairs, figuring I'd better ice the knee. Holding a Chicken Primavera Lean Cuisine in place, I stretched out on the couch.

The red pig called.

What possessed me to pick up was beyond me. Why couldn't I have let it go to voice mail? It was a byproduct of my upbringing. My parents could never bear to let a phone ring more than three times before diving for it; across platters of Wiener schnitzels, sleeping cats and a grandparent or two.

"Hey, Rupe ..." Her assumed familiarity offended me. It was a transparent attempt at faux neighborliness. She must want something. "There are black kids in the lobby."

"Yeah."

"It's bad for the building."

"In what way?"

"I shouldn't have to spell it out for you."

I wanted to make her spell it out. "I'm not sure what you mean."

"You know how these things go ..."

"What things?" I played stupid.

"One thing always leads to another."

"I'm not sure what 'these things' you're talking about are."

She whispered. "They're black."

"Oh, you mean LoKey's kids?"

"I knew it. We're done for. There's no stopping

it now. Pretty soon it'll be gangs ... the building gets tagged ... burglarized ... I might get raped ..."

That definitely wasn't happening.

"Brenda, don't worry about it."

"Easy for you to say. And that Mo-nique is making a racket, clicking her car alarm all the time."

"She has a right to turn on her car alarm."

"It's an echo chamber back there. I can't take it."

"I don't know what to say. This is apartment living."

"On top of everything, Mikey's been kidnapped."

"What?" I acted like I had no prior knowledge.

"He's so beautiful. I'm sure one of the tenants snatched him. They're all selfish bastards."

"If you get a ransom note, let me know." I hung up.

Sometime later, having passed out, I woke to the sound of beans being ground at the Armenian coffee shop. Damn, my hearing was sharp today. I often wondered about my range of hearing. Some days, it was like the elderlies and I could barely make out the operator's instructions while on hold with my cable provider. But then, inexplicably, at other times, it was almost shark-like. But was it on a par with Aquaman's?

While in the midst of a further side-by-side comparison with Aquaman and our various traits, I heard a faint knock at the door. The Lean Cuisine had done its job well. I leapt up, barely wincing from my morning's injuries, to find Don waiting.

"I was getting worried. I was knocking for a long time."

"I didn't hear you."

"I'm sorry to bother you ... I found this in the

lobby. I took it down."

Don handed me a note. The handwriting was unmistakable. While I recovered from my on-the-job injuries, the red pig had penned a libelous screed. She'd used a Sharpie, bright orange. Why not red?

ACTUAL RED PIG NOTE:

Our "Do nothing Manager"

let's tenants do as they please.

He's inconsiderate of others. This

was once a quite building. Neighbourly.

Not anymore.

I was surprised and pleased to see that "nothing" was correctly written in lowercase, it being used in its adverbial form. And I had to give Brenda credit, whether thought-out or simply an off-the-cuff rallying cry, the "Our" in the opening was a nice touch. But there was no context to the "he's inconsiderate" smear. She'd called me out for not sharing her "white fright" over two black children playing Bakugan in the lobby. Not to mention, the inversion of "quiet" for "quite." Was it so hard to distinguish between the two? Then again, maybe Brenda was dyslexic and I should cut her some slack. But the "u" in "neighborly" was unforgiveable. I knew Brenda wasn't British. Plus, I was being fingered for destroying a sense of community/fabled Shangri-La/simpler time gone by, i.e., when the Dryden Arms was ruled by whites.

I moved toward Don, comfortably settled on the kidney-shaped chair. "Brenda thinks the building is going downhill. What was it like when you first moved in?"

"She was a troublemaker from the start. Always

complaining. Didn't like this one or that one. The building's gotten much nicer the last few years. Most of the bad eggs are gone."

Except for Brenda and Marie.

I was hungry. "Don, how about joining me for dinner?"

"What do you have?"

"There was a sale at Ralphs on Lean Cuisines. I'm stocked. I got it all. Chicken Primavera—I held up the make-do icepack—Beef Chow Fun, Mushroom Mezzaluna Ravioli, Tortilla Crusted Fish and Stuffed Cabbage. I'll make them all."

"For dessert?"

"Trader Joe's soy ice cream sandwiches. Chocolate and vanilla."

"I'll stay."

As I headed for the freezer, Don took stock of my place. "You have a nice view."

"Not as nice as yours."

"True. But I'm just happy to have a window."

It was a veritable feast. I'd prepared two each of my top-four favorite Lean Cuisine entrées. The kitchen table was packed.

Peeling back the last of the plastic coverings, we dug in. Don had a good appetite. It was nice to see him enjoying himself.

"What was that place without a window?"

"I had a nice boss. He gave me a cot in the store's basement."

"How'd you make your meals?"

"There was a hot plate down there."

"Was that hard?"

"I did okay."

We ate in silence for a little while.

"I heard from the Magician that you're a writer." Don said.

"I was."

"But not now?"

"It's hard to explain."

"You can tell me."

"It started when both my parents died. I wrote about it. It helped heal me. It was everything to me."

"That's good."

"But I lost it."

"How could that happen?"

"I was sentimental and used my mother's old Underwood typewriter. It helped me get it out. When I finally finished it, I was bringing it to my English professor for notes. He was a big supporter of mine. I was on the A-train heading uptown when these two rough-looking guys started hassling an older couple. They shoved the husband against the doors. The wife cried for help as they ripped her purse from her arm and ran out the next set of subway doors, as they opened. I chased after them to get the purse back, through the gate, and up the stairs to street level. I lost them in the sea of people. And my only copy of that novel was on that train. I tried to track it down through the MTA, posted reward notices, ads in the local papers. I'm sure it ended up in the trash."

"I'm sorry about that, Rupert."

We sat quietly eating our Trader Joe's soy ice cream bars, both chocolate and vanilla. I managed to shape a wrapper into a sticky airplane.

"Can I see that Internet now?"

"Sure. Let me show you."

Later that night, I crawled into bed comforted by my worn-in Spidey pajamas—a consolation prize for not being able to locate a pair of Silver Surfer ones. Apparently, the Silver Surfer didn't have the same merchandising muscle behind him as Spidey.

I'd overdone it with the Lean Cuisines and soy ice cream sandwiches. They were getting to me, but I was too lazy to get out of bed and down a few Rolaids. I thought, *Do I just lie here and suffer? Should I get up?* Decisions. I hated making them late at night. Everything always seemed grimmer after 10:00-10:30 p.m. But my stomach hurt ...

CRASH! SCREAM! MORE CRASHING! ANOTHER SCREAM!

Well, now I HAD to get up.

DATE	TRANSACTION DESCRIPTION	PAYMENT, FEE, WITHDRAWAL (-)	✓	DEPOSIT, CREDIT (+)	$
4.16.15	Lean Cuisines, contact lens solution, Q-tips	46.09			1,947.87
4.17.15	Trader Joe's soy ice cream sandwiches and tangelos	19.43			1,928.44

14

I couldn't shake the horrific image of Marie in her granny nightgown, wig askew, screaming at me from her doorway last night.

"I could have been killed you fucking asshole!" Had been her initial greeting.

I'd surveyed the wreckage over her shoulder, a tuft of wig hair obscuring my line of sight. But I'd still seen where the ceiling had come crashing down in her bedroom, inches from the foot of her bed. A few chunks of ceiling had actually landed on the bottom left corner, a near miss for her stubby, block feet.

"This building is shit! I hate you all!"

"If you'd let us in to fix that leak when it first started, we wouldn't be such a bunch of shitty assholes. And you wouldn't be under a pile of ceiling. I'll be back with Herman the plumber, first thing in the morning."

"Drop dead!" She slammed the door in my face.

With the rising sun, Herman and I approached Marie's door as a two-man paid militia—at least Herman was being paid. While I wielded a *fifty*-foot roll of heavy-duty Reynolds Wrap, Herman shouldered a baseball bat–sized flashlight. We were ready to rumble. I knocked.

"Get the fuck away from my door!" It remained bolted shut. A night's sleep amidst plaster, dust and lead paint hadn't softened Marie's mood.

"But Marie, I have Reynolds Wrap. The heavy-duty kind. *Fifty*-feet of it."

"Are you deaf?"

"My hearing is excellent."

"Then maybe you just don't speak English, you idiot."

"Well, technically German was my first language. My parents were ..."

"I don't give a shit."

"Ma'am." Herman jumped in to arbitrate. "We need to get in and have a quick look. A few minutes of your time."

"No ... one ... comes ... in."

"Ma'am, this is a critical maintenance issue ..."

"Fuck off!"

Herman and I retreated. Bald lady in nasty granny nightgown: 1. Me and super-plumber Herman: 0.

"I'm gonna have to bring out the big guns on this one. It's time to get Larry involved."

"You'd better. We've got a plumbing crisis on our hands. If they don't start re-piping soon, the foundation could flood. That's a minimum of $50,000."

We moved upstairs, I dialed. Me on the kidney-shaped chair, Herman crouched by my side, we leaned in to the iPhone speaker resting on my Eames knock-off coffee table. It was our version of the Situation Room, minus the Secret Service presence, minus high-tech audio-visuals, minus real-time digital mapping and sadly, minus the Krispy Kremes.

Larry was silent as I debriefed him, Herman peppering in plumbing prognostications. Then,

"Herman, can we avoid re-piping?"

"Sir, that ship has sailed."

I was happy to hear Herman harken back to the building's nautical roots.

"I ... um ..." Long pause. "Gentlemen, I must patch in Duncan Danforth."

Was it my imagination or had the stress of the situation caused Larry's carefully hidden German accent to creep out? I could picture the sweat gathering and forming into large beads on his upper lip. Adding to my suspicions, Larry's hold music was the idyllic Muzak version of Disney's *It's a Small World*, which any musicologist could tell you sprung from the Wagnerian school.

"I have Duncan Danforth on the line. Duncan ..."

"I'm here ... fill me in."

"Herman is saying the foundation could flood!" I sounded a bit hysterical.

"Let's start from the beginning." Duncan was in control.

Herman and I recounted the events vis-à-vis the Marie affair. Herman went on to further detail in grim tones the global nature of the plumbing problem we were facing. The Marie ceiling collapse was no one-off. It was a harbinger of things to come.

There was silence on the line. Had Duncan fainted, Larry taken a cyanide capsule? What was happening? I was confused. Finally ...

"Herman, can you buy us some time before we're underwater?" Duncan asked.

"Jet the lines and keep snaking." Larry chimed in.

"The pipes are crumbling. But, yes sir!" Herman was on it.

I guess it was on me to remind everyone about

the standoff we were having with Marie. "Gentlemen," (copy-catting Larry's style), "how do we solve the problem of Marie-a?" Had I just sung a line from one of my all-time favorite childhood movies, *The Sound of Music*?

"Yes, that is one foul-mouthed lady," Herman said.

"Marie's been nothing but trouble for years," Larry agreed.

"She's going to have to shape up or ship out, she's not running things here! I'll draft an applicable letter. We're in charge."

I wanted to jump up and down and clap my hands and run through the apartment skipping rope, the joy was too much. But I thought it best not to let Herman see that particular side of me.

"Rupert, Herman, thanks for your time, good work. Larry, please stay on the line."

I felt exhilarated. Marie was finally gonna get hers. I flashed on black & white images of Marie in an ill-fitting trench coat, kerchief tied over her wig, on the run through a dark, rain-soaked alley, tripping over garbage cans and trying to avoid rats—like herself.

Leading Herman out, I transitioned my film noir fantasy to the final confrontation between Fred McMurray and Barbara Stanwyck in Billy Wilder's classic *Double Indemnity*. Stanwyck, like Marie, was a baaaddd woman. Once I got Duncan Danforth's letter, I could deliver it to Marie with the same vengeance in my heart that McMurray delivered those final gunshots to Stanwyck. "Goodbye, baby," he'd said. I'd say, "How about a one-way trip to the Greyhound bus station?"

As Herman headed for his van, I stood in the doorway facing a strange man scrolling through the list of names on the security panel. He was dressed like a young Republican or sports commentator making me particularly suspicious.

"Can I help you?"

"Yeah. I'm looking for a Mr. Rupert ..."

"Oh, my God! I knew it. I knew it. I finally won the Publishers Clearing House Sweepstakes."

All that hard work paid off. I'd been relentlessly mailing back entries and spending most of my disposable income on their magazine subscriptions. I couldn't wait to get my hands on that giant check.

"Wait, is the film crew here?"

"Actually, I'm with the L.A. Superior Court. You've been served."

He slapped a folded piece of paper in my hand, and dashed off. This was almost as good as winning the Sweepstakes. Ever since my obsession with watching all things *Law & Order*, it'd been a dream of mine to testify at a trial. I rushed back to 204, settled on the kidney-shaped chair, and tore open the paper.

I was required to appear for Eli's preliminary hearing. It'd be my chance to live amongst the underbelly of society. Except I'd have to bring an insulated soft cooler with snacks, not trusting the hygiene of the courthouse cafeteria food. Gangbangers were known to disregard the salad bar sneeze-guards. Shifty lawyers with their God complexes always fingered the mini-Kaiser rolls with impunity. I was sickened.

But I was determined to blend in with the scum. I'd be slumped over on a hard wooden bench, gnawing on baby carrots and string cheese, and every so often would cough up a loogie and spit it on the floor, establishing solidarity with the snorting, wheezing pimp-daddies, skin-picking junkies and sharkskin-suited Medicare fraudsters.

Wait a minute. I was totally unprepared for the vicious cross-examination I'd surely be subject to from Eli's squat, balding, whiny-voiced Jew lawyer, if not from the hot-looking Angie Harmon–type D.A. leaning over me in the witness box, cleavage peeking out from her understated, cream-colored silk blouse.

First order of business was to make sure I was in the clear and in no way culpable for Eli's actions. I needed to establish that I'd simply been an innocent bystander fearing for my life. I'd better jot down MY VERSION of the story, so I didn't forget. I jogged my memory for the specifics of the night in question. I recalled every single detail all the way through Eli's love of baked goods. After all, I was prepping for trial.

I'd need to incorporate the post-shooting accounts—by way of Hat Guy, who actually didn't see a thing—and then cross-reference those with actual eyewitnesses—Jonas and Astrid. I wouldn't allow for the possibility of other testimony leading to a *Rashomon* scenario, distorting the timeline and veracity of my own account.

What if a tenant cabal was underway to oust me? A unified, counter version of the Eli situation might place me in a suspicious light. Would it lead to criminal charges?

I wrote up tenant profiles and examples showing the unreliability of their words and actions. I'd be ready to puncture holes in any lies they told on the stand.

After a thorough review of my notes, I constructed a narrative of events, a story that was impenetrable, no matter the efforts of a tenant cabal, Angie Harmon or the Jew lawyer to break me on the stand.

Life experience and the hard realities of managing the Dryden Arms had led to an evolution in my literary style. There was an honesty and integrity to my prose that was in fact gripping. When the time came, I'd blow the roof off that L.A. County courthouse.

It'd been a rich, exciting and satisfying morning. I surely deserved a special treat. It was time to nuke two of those four-cheese cannelloni Lean Cuisine I'd been saving for a special occasion. Today was the day.

Placing the tray in the microwave reminded me of the cafeteria food from P.S. 6, served in a similar container. It's where I spent first through sixth grades. The food had been peppered with sedatives. I was sure of it. How else could the teachers have kept overcrowded classrooms packed with hyperactive kids under control? I had proof! What other explanation could there be for having virtually no memories from that time. Clearly, I'd been drugged. I was Ray Milland from *The Lost Weekend.*

Propelled by the unadulterated cannelloni, I took a closer look at the language of my narrative. Absolute clarity was a must. There couldn't be any ambiguity whatsoever. Word choice would prove crucial. Structure was paramount. It's a shame I couldn't share the finished product with Brenda, as a teaching tool for her future attack-driven notes.

Drawing on my copywriting experience for the unnamable—due to my concern for legal repercussions—large hotel chain that wasn't the InterContinental Hotels Group, Wyndham Hotel Group, Accor, Choice Hotels or Best Western—I punched up the narrative, line by line, word by word, vowel combination by vowel combination.

As I was in the process of deciding on the word *perfidious* or *treacherous* to describe Marie's base character, the power went out. I'd been too enthralled with the sweeping nature of my tale to hit SAVE.

It was lost.

Regardless, I was on the job. Channeling Matt the laundry repair guy, I moved with a steely resolve and checked the unit's circuit breakers: all good. I then cut a swath through the darkness led only by my significantly smaller than Herman's flashlight, to the individual apartment breakers in the basement. I didn't know what I was looking for. I called Vasco. Voice mail full.

There was a shock waiting outside my door. The flashlight landed on the Orc's face. His normal angry expression had evolved into something worse—fear. There was nothing more unnatural than a frightened Orc.

"I did it."

"Did what?"

"Blew the power, man."

"You blew the electricity in the whole building? How?"

"Maybelline wouldn't let me hire a gaffer."

"A what?"

"Like a movie electrician guy."

"You're making a movie in your unit?"

"That's what we do man. I plugged that damn light in and it blew everything. Every minute we're down, we're losing money."

"How's that?"

"Live subscribers."

"This disaster made me lose the only real writing I've done in years. You're not the only one losing here."

That snapped the Orc out of his state.

"Man, I can't believe that. I know how hard that is. Concepting story lines for these web-casts is killing me. I'm so sorry."

The next thing I knew, I was enveloped in the Orc's arms. The hug was awkward, yet strangely cathartic. I felt better. After being released from our embrace, I was ready to tackle the outage.

"I'll get us back up and running."

"Thanks, bro."

I was putting the keys in the door, when I felt something behind me. The ghost? "Come upstairs with me. I don't want to be alone in the dark." It was Judy.

"I would but I've gotta get on the lights."

"I'm sure there's some time to kill before the electrician gets here."

"I'm still waiting for Vasco to get back to me."

"Vasco? He's not an electrician."

"But he knows the building."

"Are you kidding? We need a real electrician. Not some illegal that crossed the border with a pair of pliers, duct tape and a bottle of tequila."

I was annoyed. But she did have a valid point. Vasco was a drunk illegal who might light us on fire.

"Okay. I'll find an electrician."

"Then you'll come upstairs. We can wait it out together."

I couldn't be with Judy. No matter the benefits.

"Judy ... I'm just not ..."

"Better get on that electrician situation. We're good." I hoped we were.

She ran her fingers through the front of my hair, much like Streisand's gloved hand ran through Redford's golden locks at the choke-back-the-tears moment of *The Way We Were*.

Checking the vendor list, Vasco was listed under

electrician. But I dug around for that flyer left on the front door knob. It advertised a licensed, bonded electrician. Troy was the man. From his picture on the flyer, he looked capable.

Within ninety seconds, Troy returned my call and was en route. Knowing that licensed, bonded help was on the way, I soldiered on recreating the Eli narrative on a legal-sized legal-pad.

What was that? Was I hearing things—God knows I could—or was Brenda calling out for Mikey? It was coming from a distance. The sound of her voice came closer. I could hear it: "Mikey ... Mikey ..." What was she doing in the hallway? Sounded like she was going door to door calling for him. She honestly believed that Mikey was being held hostage in one of the apartments by one of his admirers or one of her enemies, and that the sound of her voice would cause him to find the strength to wrestle free from his gag and restraints and meow loudly, alerting her to his whereabouts. It'd only been a day. But to Mikey, it may have been weeks.

Three hours later, Troy handed me a hefty bill. But it was lights on again at the Dryden Arms. Apparently, the winds of Glendale had knocked neutral off the transformer on a telephone pole. So, it wasn't the Orc. I'd let him know, to assuage his feelings of guilt.

As Troy's van receded in the distance, I heard a loud *POP* and everything went black. The entire neighborhood—if not all of Glendale—plunged into darkness. What the hell happened here? Troy!

He'd been up to something. You know, I'd never seen an electrician that good-looking or well dressed. He was more like those Euro-trash criminals in the vein of Alan Rickman and his crew from the first *Die Hard* movie. I was willing to bet Troy had been laying in wait for an emergency electrical call close enough to the Nestlé corporate offices right up the street, so he and his good-looking "electrician friends" could rig a citywide power outage and be left poised to grab the priceless, secret recipe for both regular and strawberry Nesquik. And probably those delicious Tollhouse cookies too. It was genius.

My phone was instantly flooded with calls and texts.

The Orc: "I didn't do it this time."

Judy: "Great electrician."

Monique: "What happened?"

Jonas: "What the fuck, Rupe?"

Hat Guy: "Should I call Ronnie?"

Astrid (or the roommate): "How long will this take?"

Marie: "Motherfucker!"

Hat Guy: "Dude. This could be the whole Western Grid. Man, we're fucked. Where are you?"

"Out front."

Marie charged through the front door. "What the hell have you been doing?"

"Working with a licensed, bonded electrician."

"I was in the middle of watching *America's Got Talent*. Now, I'm gonna miss the second-graders doing *Les Mis* tonight."

Who knew she had a soft spot for young children. It was those smelly middle-schoolers who'd scarred her.

"Rupert, my Breyers is melting." Brenda yelled down from her window, shining a flashlight straight into my eyes.

"Everyone be calm."

"Dude, there's gonna be looting." Hat Guy

emerged, a miner's headlamp wrapped around his pork pie hat.

"Fuck this!" Marie stormed back in, stomping her little block feet.

Passing Marie, LoKey strode out cool as ever, in full Puma regalia.

"'Sup, bra?"

"Trying to keep the tenants calm."

"Smoke?" Hat Guy offered LoKey a cigarette.

LoKey looked impressed with the headlamp as he accepted. They lit up.

"Rupert, Rupert. Are those Armenian kids gonna come for us?"

I looked up at Brenda, who eyed LoKey, the real source of her fear.

"Stay inside, keep your door locked." Brenda slammed her window shut.

As Hat Guy and LoKey dragged on their smokes, I was thinking about Troy and what my next move should be.

Hat Guy: "I saw her today."

Me: "Who?"

Hat Guy: "The roommate."

LoKey: "Whose roommate?"

Hat Guy: "Astrid's."

LoKey: "I didn't know she had a roommate."

Me: "She doesn't."

Hat Guy: "Yes, she does."

LoKey: "Should we take shifts watching the door?"

Hat Guy: "Nah. I've got us covered. Ronnie's on

his way over with a couple of baseball bats and A&W root beers."

LoKey: "I don't understand this roommate thing."

Hat Guy: "Dude, I totally saw her. She was waiting for the Blue Bus."

LoKey: "I've seen Astrid on the Blue Bus."

Me: "Astrid has a car. Why would she take the Blue Bus?"

Hat Guy: "My point exactly."

DATE	TRANSACTION DESCRIPTION	PAYMENT, FEE, WITHDRAWAL (-)	✓	DEPOSIT, CREDIT (+)	$
4.18.15	Cable speed upgrade	14.99			1,913.45

15

"See, THE LORD is coming out of his dwelling to punish the people of the earth for their sins. The earth will disclose the blood shed upon her; she will conceal her slain no longer." *Isaiah 26:21*

In reality, it was only ME, RUPERT THE MANAGER, from my dwelling, 204, acting on behalf of a higher power, Larry and Duncan Danforth, to deliver Marie her Day of Reckoning in the form of a fateful "Cease and Desist" letter.

It had taken a week for Duncan Danforth's lawyer or a $29 *LegalZoom* document to materialize. Whoever crafted it knew what they were doing. The language was absolute. Which was good. If word of its existence leaked out within the tenant community or copies were distributed, it would put them on notice that management would not tolerate any form of a rent strike, missing stairwell carpet runners, a looting of the laundry machine coin boxes or mishandling of recyclables.

In honor of the occasion, I busted open a new three-pack of Costco T-shirts, and donned the sea green one.

ACTUAL NOTICE TO PERFORM COVENANT OF LEASE OR QUIT—A "CEASE AND DESIST" LETTER IN LAYMAN'S TERMS—LEFT UNDER MARIE DE LUCA'S DOOR THE MORNING OF APRIL 25, 2015:

To Marie De Luca, tenant in possession of premises located at 1105 Kedge Road, Apartment 102, Glendale, California 91207:

You are in breach of the Rental Agreement dated December 15, 1988 (including the Rules and Regulations that are a part thereof) in that you are acting in a manner that interferes with the right of landlord to make necessary repairs and improvements to the building, interferes with the comforts and conveniences of other persons, disturbs and annoys other persons, and annoys and interferes with other residents, and in that you are talking loudly and disturbing other residents in the common areas between the hours of 10 p.m. and 9 a.m. Your words and actions are making it difficult for landlord to make plumbing repairs to the building and to make repairs to other units in the building, which landlord has the right to do.

Within three (3) days after service of this notice, you must discontinue such interferences, disturbances and annoyances, or deliver possession of the premises to the landlord's authorized agent. Your failure to perform the covenant breached as specified above, or to vacate the premises within three (3) days, will cause the undersigned to initiate legal proceedings against you to declare a forfeiture of your Rental Agreement, to recover possession of the premises, and to seek judgment for damages for each day of occupancy after the expiration date of this notice, any statutory damages and costs, and attorney fees.

You are further notified that the undersigned elects to declare the forfeiture of the Rental Agreement under which you hold possession of the premises if you fail to perform as indicated above.

Date: ________ ________________________

Duncan Danforth, Danforth LLC

Yeah. Eat that, Marie.

That being said, I always was and would be a class act. I still went to pick up Marie's paper, despite the acrimonious nature of our relationship.

Next up was grabbing Don for our video store outing. Rather than be annoyed and pace the hallway during the inevitable wait, I performed *The New York Times'* well-received 7-minute workout. As I was in my second series of lunges, the door opened.

Don was skeletal. His eyes were sunken and he was unsteady on his feet. I hoped my face didn't show how alarmed I was.

"Don ... are you okay?"

"I have an iron deficiency. I'm fine."

"Maybe we should go another time."

He braced himself in the doorway. "Can you take me to the market?

"I can go for you."

"No. I need to go."

"Um ... okay."

Don slid some change, loose bills and thin and crumbling coupons off a side table, and slowly stuffed them in his pants pocket.

Knowing Don wouldn't accept my help getting down the stairs, I jumped in front to catch him if he fell. He held on to the handrails with both hands.

To negotiate the lobby, Don silently took hold of my arm. It was an ordeal getting him out of the building and into my car. He struggled to pull the seatbelt across.

"Ah, it gets stuck all the time." I wanted to preserve some of his dignity.

We hit the market sometime after the housewives were done with the morning's carpools. It was me, Don and a bunch of moderately aggressive soccer moms gliding through the aisles. We had to watch out for the ones on their cell phones.

Don gripped the side of our shopping cart as I eased it along.

"So ... um ... when was the last time you went to the doctor?"

"Not sure."

"You've got Medicare, right?"

"I don't know about that."

I bet Don paid out-of-pocket and couldn't afford to go back, even if he wanted to.

"It pays for you to go to the doctor, so it's free. You should get it."

"I don't want to burden anyone."

"No. Every retired person is entitled to it. I can't wait to get it." Making those COBRA payments every month was a killer.

Don mumbled to himself. "I need Ragu spaghetti sauce."

"Let's go to the free clinic."

"Where's the Campbell's soup?"

I'd have to put some thought into this one.

After lightly filling the cart, we moved to the checkout stand. Don's fingers shook as he handed over the coupons and some loose change.

"Ralphs card?" The checker asked.

Don looked embarrassed. Without a phone number, he couldn't get one.

I punched in my number for the discount.

Riding back in silence, Don leaning his head against the window, I saw that the series of flyers with a hand-drawn picture of Mikey were water-stained and torn. They'd been the handiwork of Lamar and DeAndre—free of the misspellings and grammatical abominations that littered the red pig's notes. BRING MIKEY BACK TO HIS HOME. NO QUESTIONS ASKED. CASH MONEY PAID and a phone number was all it said. There were also enticing images of moneybags with the $ symbol on them. The boys had gone through round after round of sketches on the stone benches out front, making use of crayons, charcoal and watercolors. They managed to capture a softened version of Mikey's image. Gone was the pissed off, menacing, real-life persona, replaced by a forlorn, hopeful expression. The use of color and shadowing was an accomplishment.

On either side of the street, Mikey's face was plastered on every freestanding object. It was hard to feel sorry for someone like Brenda. But she was alone, and he was the only thing she really loved.

After settling Don in his apartment and making him some Campbell's Chicken & Stars soup—even though he said he could manage it—I left. My nerves were shot. Seeing Don like that had gotten to me. Did he have anybody? He didn't seem to have much money. It was sad to be old, sick and alone.

Had I been too quick to dismiss Judy? After all, we were both alone. It's nice to have someone.

I was starting to feel melancholy. I'd pick up my spirits by checking if Marie took in her letter.

She had! I felt better.

Acting on Don's behalf, I pulled out his brittle, yellowed rental application to see if there was someone I didn't know about. The only person listed was a Mr. Otto Berman of Monrovia, California, owner of Berman's Pharmacy. Don had been the deliveryman there for nineteen years. When I called Berman's number, it now belonged to a P.F. Chang's. The only Otto Berman I found on Google was a long-dead mobster. Was that why Don was so cryptic about his past?

Regardless, I couldn't let Don go under. Since I had his Social Security number, I went on the Medicare site, but it was a complicated situation. I called them up.

I was number eighteen in the queue, when thoughts of Maybelline slipping off her silk robe unspooled in my mind. I wondered if there was enough time to tug one out. When she started fondling her breasts, I was twelfth. I couldn't chance it.

It was a bit rough when I got Medicare on the line. The woman was ready to hang up on me, when she heard I wasn't a relative. I had to do some fast-talking to have her hear me out. After explaining that Don was sick and alone and too proud to do this for himself, I got to her. By the end of the call, I was an expert in all things Medicare and knew exactly what paperwork needed to be filed. I just had to get Don on board.

Mini-cannoli, chocolate covered and plain. Don had a sweet tooth and I wasn't above pandering.

It was either the Campbell's Chicken & Stars or the sugar from the cannoli that gave Don a boost. He had more color in his face.

Don was on his wing chair, halfway into his third cannolo, me perched on the edge of his open, unmade Murphy bed making a stronger pitch to sign him up for Medicare. I was hoping the cannoli would soften his stance.

"You just have to sign these few papers and it's done."

Don looked distracted. I assumed by who was going to get the last cannolo.

"I'm concerned about something."

"You can have the last cannolo."

"That's not what I mean."

"Remember, there's no cost to enroll."

"I'm worried about Marie."

"Marie?"

"She's in real trouble, Rupert."

Why would he care? She only ever complained about him and his walking.

"I didn't know you two were friendly."

"We've been neighbors for thirty years."

"But she's so mean."

"She's not all that bad."

"Yes, she is."

"She's had a lot of trouble in her life."

"Of her own making, I'd bet."

"That might be. But I don't want to see her out on the street. Her money's running out, she got laid-off from the school district, and her unemployment is over. If she loses this rent-controlled apartment, where will she go?"

To hell. I hoped.

"Why can't she cooperate?"

"She's always been ornery, that one."

"It's really up to her. No one's pushing her out."

Don looked worried. He knew she wasn't going to change.

I made a little more progress with Don, as we split the last cannolo. But he was still reluctant to put pen to paper. For my next visit, I'd be armed with Cinnabons. He'd definitely sign.

The sugar had amped me up. To keep the rush going, the Magician and I could hit those donut shops.

He wasn't home. But Hat Guy was out front either still on patrol, or performing more unauthorized lawn care. Maybe I could mooch an A&W root beer off him.

Hat Guy was in deep thought, staring at I don't know what.

"Any A&Ws left over from the other night?"

"What? Maybe. I'll have to check. Wait. Have you seen this?"

"Seen what?"

"The bark hasn't been treated. You need bark that doesn't destroy plants, so they can breathe ... dude, check this out. I bought a hand-held edge trimmer." Hat Guy held it up with pride, and then leaned across me and clipped a few brown spots off a Juniper bush. "No more scissors, dude."

"What's the point, man?"

"Are you kidding? They're sharper and totally precise."

"Not the trimmer. Is it inevitable we just grow old, decline and die alone?"

"You're bringing me down, man."

"Sorry. It's the headspace I'm in right now. A lot of heavy stuff's been going on."

"And always will. Dammit! I told De Soto he

needs to stake the bushes. They're fucking dying. Not that he gives a shit. I'm gonna save these bushes myself."

Hat Guy crushed his cigarette out against a paving stone, pocketed it and did a quick perusal of the lawn. He dug a toe under a pile of bark, kicked it, and turned to me, with a curious smile.

"Let's get this straight. They HAVE different colored bark ... green-gray stuff that goes with wooden trellises ... it's the obvious choice. It's gonna happen."

"Any chance of that A&W before death takes me?" I still had the sugar shakes.

"Speaking of death, I found that piece of shit white cat."

"Mikey?"

"What was left of him. I was checking the succulents by the garages. Coyotes."

"What'd you do with him?"

"Dumpster."

"Ooo ... that's a tough way to go. How are we gonna tell Brenda? That cat was her life."

"I'll write her a note."

DATE	TRANSACTION DESCRIPTION	PAYMENT, FEE, WITHDRAWAL (-)	✓	DEPOSIT, CREDIT (+)	$
4.25.15	Mini-cannoli, (chocolate and plain)	23.09			1,890.36

16

"Pick a card."

I thought the Magician would never ask. At some point, I worried the fancy shuffling, deck-cutting and more fancy shuffling was actually the whole trick. It was a good thing I could distract myself with my Challah-style French toast.

I pulled out my pocket-sized hand sanitizer to make sure my fingers were free of sticky syrup before zeroing in on the jack of hearts.

"Now put it back," the Magician commanded. Our waitress, Lynette according to her badge, who looked like she'd been at this establishment since Mildred Pierce's pie place closed in '45, took in the show.

I wedged the Jack seven-eighths off to the right side of the deck to see if I could throw the Magician off the scent.

More shuffling ensued as I polished off the French toast. At last, the cards were fanned directly in front of me. One of the cards was pushed out from the rest.

"This your card?" It was the eight of clubs.

Triumphantly. "No ..."

His face a mask, the Magician reached into his mouth and pulled out a crumpled, saliva-soaked card. My card.

"Oh, my God! How'd you do that?" Lynette squealed.

"All right, so you're a real magician."

"Master of the riffle shuffle."

"Cool."

Lynette topped of our coffees, and scampered off.

"I wish you were coming on this tour with me. Those show broads ..." He gestured a curvaceous woman with his hands and busted out a pop and whistle noise.

"All I've had is that tonguing from Judy."

"... I'm gonna have two on each arm. Its more than one magician can handle."

"I'll miss you."

"The road's calling and I'm listening."

"Why don't you keep your place?"

"Glendale is played out. I need to see where this takes me."

"Who else is gonna kick my ass?"

"As long as you're writing, you'll be fine. You are writing, right?"

"I'm living, breathing it all the time. I'm gathering material, as we speak."

"Cut the crap, Rupert."

"It's the building. It pulls my focus."

"Forget it, Rupert. It's Chinatown."

"But we're in Glendale."

The Magician shook his head and with a slice of bread, mopped up a puddle of egg yolk from his plate.

My phone dinged.

Hat Guy: "Dude. I just saw the roommate run

into the building."

The Magician sighed. "I'm plagued by this Mikey thing."

"We all are the circle of life."

"If I hadn't propped that door open ..."

Hat Guy text number two: "Dude. You there?"

"It was his time."

"You're right." The Magician looked down and pondered his hash browns for a moment.

Hat Guy text number three: "I saw a light go on in Astrid's place. DUDE! CALL ME!"

The Magician turned to me. "'Death is nothing, but to live defeated and inglorious is to die daily'."

"Napoleon?"

"I don't know. Some dictator."

Post-breakfast, reclining in the kidney-shaped chair, I started responding to the backlog of Hat Guy texts. Not wanting to speak to him directly, I used the iPhone 6 Plus as a buffer. The Corleone family had a lot of buffers. I only had one.

During a lull in the text exchange, there was a weird clawing, rapping sound at the door. Marie.

"I bet you're happy."

We had a momentary stare-down.

"No thanks to you, I have to move back to Astoria. In with my mother."

I imagined a short, shriveled, Sicilian version of Lady Macbeth.

I had no sympathy. "How soon are you leaving?"

"End of the month. Soon enough for you?"

"Sure. Don't forget to slide the keys under my

door with a forwarding address. I'll mail your security deposit within twenty-one days."

"Fat chance. You'll give it to me, before I leave."

"That's not how it works. We need to do a move-out inspe ..."

"Don't fuck with me. My cousin Artie is a lawyer. He'll shit down your throat."

Wanting to sever all ties and never have to deal with Marie again, I'd pay her off in petty cash from my discretionary fund. She'd lived here so long her deposit was probably about a hundred bucks.

"No need for cousin Artie. I'll cash you out." I closed the door on her.

In my role as Resident Manager, I'd take the next logical step. Marie's apartment would need a deep cleansing—primarily spiritual—but with a strong-smelling all-purpose cleaner too. Cortez and Vasco could handle the all-purpose cleaner part. Not having a Native American shaman on my vendor list, I'd take a trip out to one of the Indian casinos near Palm Springs to find one.

Once at the casino, I'd slip a Native bus boy a couple twenties to shake out info on who the top shamans in town were. But that could be awkward. They might think I was looking for sex or meth. If I wasn't careful, I could wind up offending someone and end up in the casino's walk-in cooler—covered in chicken feathers—a victim of a terrible misunderstanding. To play it safe, I'd go to Amazon and order an extra-large bundle of sage and burn it in Marie's place.

Before signing in to my Amazon account, I wanted to see how Don was doing. I also wanted to do something about that busted-out chair of his. I'd reassign one of the unused lobby chairs to Don's unit. I didn't want to sit on that Murphy bed anymore. He'd accept it more easily, if I made it about me.

Chair parked outside Don's front door, I decided to sit in it during my inevitable extended wait. There'd be no lunges today. Towing the chair up to the third-floor had been enough of a workout.

Don never opened up. He must have been out or taking a nap. I'd do the same. Nap that is: in the manager's residence.

That Challah-style French toast put me down. I unzipped my jeans, leaned back on the couch, and was gone.

Before I knew it, I found myself spotlighted in front of a packed audience. Small-club intimacy. Kind of dingy. There was a cooler stocked with ice-cold beer on the floor, next to my falling apart armchair. I'd popped open my sixth can of Schlitz, giving a Bukowski-style reading. Cheers followed every beer I downed—wild hollering. We were in a communal experience, until the mood turned ugly.

There was yelling from the back. Drunks challenged me to fight. I couldn't quite make them out. But I recognized their voices.

Marie: "I'm gonna shit down your throat."

Brenda: "You're a thief, just like Vasco."

Jonas: "I can't hear you." He started stomping around and tossed a beer bottle right past my ear.

Events spiraled out of control. More beer bottles whooshed past my head. Hat Guy feathered green-gray bark across the lawn. Cortez slit a rooster's throat.

Eli: "I have something for you." BANG! BANG!

The sound was deafening. What the hell? I must have been out for hours. It was dark and raining outside and the banging persisted.

Zipping up my jeans, I went to the window to see what was going on. The palm fronds were flailing in strong gusts of wind. Since I didn't see anything awry on the street, and the banging seemed like it was coming from above, I headed for the roof, stopping at the hallway closet to select which of my raincoats was right for the occasion. I went with the hooded one. It was thin, but bright enough to be spotted in the event of an emergency.

Stepping onto the roof, I propped open the fire door with a rusty paint can and was immediately pummeled in the face by wind and rain. None of my raincoats were substantive enough to deal with this kind of weather. I'd have to rethink my collection.

Whipping out my smallish flashlight, I scanned the rooftop. The light from the flashlight was dimmer than my iPhone 6 Plus's, but I didn't want to risk water damage. I was still under contract.

Through the dim light, wind and rain, I could see that one of the 18 HVAC (heating, ventilation, air-conditioning) units had come unbolted and was thrashing around, tethered to the building only by the cables running down to the unit it was connected to.

It looked precarious, and I was worried the fucker might break free, fly off the building and take someone out on the street below. I texted and made some calls. I got voice mails and no response. It was on me.

I had it. Timing it like Steve McQueen's raft escape in *Papillion*, I waited for the wind to settle, and as the HVAC unit landed, I pounced.

My plan worked. I was sitting on top of the HVAC. Now what? It was secure. But I had no plan beyond this. If I got up, the HVAC would start thrashing around again. I'd sit there until inspiration struck, or someone called back.

Sitting on the HVAC, jeans getting soaked, it was apparent that my raincoat collection was lacking. I needed to go shopping. REI, Eddie Bauer, Lands' End, The North Face, L.L. Bean, Burlington Coat Factory? It would be hard to choose. I was imagining their online catalog of raincoats when a beam of light hit me square in the eyes.

"Rupert? Is that you?"

It was Judy in a maxi-length hooded raincoat—she'd stay dry. She was wielding a Black & Decker LED Alkaline Spotlight flashlight. I'd wanted one of those babies for a long time.

"Yeah. Nice flashlight."

"It was my ex's."

"What brings you up here?"

"The noise. Sounded like we were under attack."

"One of those units broke loose. I have it under control."

"How?"

"I'm sitting on it, till it's secured."

"How long's that going to take?"

"I have messages into Vasco and Larry."

"So it'll be a while."

"Probably."

"Want some company?" She was uncharacteristically unforward.

"Sure."

Judy slid onto the HVAC next to me and dialed down the brightness of her ex's flashlight. We sat there in silence for a few minutes. It didn't feel uncomfortable.

"Look what I've got." Judy held out some rolls of Smarties.

"I love those!"

"I know. They're the best."

She divvied them up, two rolls for me, one for her. Thoughtful.

"So, what's your story?" I asked.

"Recent or ancient history?"

"I want it all."

"Okay ..."

Judy drew a picture of a mill town outside Pittsburgh. Drunken father, distant mother, narcissistic sister. It was pure dysfunction. She escaped it working at a print shop after school. Reading the material that came through the shop sparked her interest in publishing. She stayed in that job long enough to save for New York, eventually landing a secretary's job at Random House. Hard work, long hours and dedication paid off. Within five years, she had twenty people working under her.

"I'm a real success story." She laughed.

"What's so funny?"

"Now, I'm a feared bitch."

"You're not as scary as I thought you were." That put a smile on her face.

"How did you wind up sitting under the Glendale sky with me tonight?"

I wondered how far back to go. To the Holocaust-surviving Jewish family, who made it to the Upper East Side of Manhattan? Or was that a sob story? Touch on my fourth-grade report on our field trip to the Central Park Zoo in which I described the seals' insouciant nature? Mrs. Karp, my teacher, called my parents in for a private conference to discuss a budding writer. It might seem boastful.

I told her everything.

"I didn't expect it to be this lonely here."

"It's like a self-imposed exile. You know, like the Silver Surfer. Except, you did it to yourself. Do you know his story? How Galactus spared the Surfer's home planet ..."

"You're the first person who understands me!"

"The parallel is clear." I had to take a moment to process what I just heard.

"Someone texted you."

It was Vasco. It was hard to hear him over what sounded like a deep-voiced Diana Ross calling out 'N-43, 4-3' in the background. Was he at drag queen bingo? In any event, Vasco took me through the steps of disconnecting the cables. With Judy's help, we carried the HVAC to the third-floor landing where it would stay, until Vasco and Cortez dealt with it.

"Thanks, Judy. You turned this into a surprisingly pleasant experience."

"It was fun. Now I need to go get dry." She turned to head to her apartment. I grabbed her hand and pulled her close. I kissed her harder than I expected.

DATE	TRANSACTION DESCRIPTION	PAYMENT, FEE, WITHDRAWAL (-)	✓	DEPOSIT, CREDIT (+)	$
5.3.15	Challah French toast breakfast special	12.99			1,877.37
5.3.15	White sage	6.49			1,870.88

17

I was lucid in the morning. The wind and rain had cleared out the SoCal smog, and my mind. There was nothing greater than waking up to a crisp, clear blue sky. Plus, I'd been laid.

I hadn't expected to like Judy this much. Underneath the vicious, cold-hearted bitch façade was a warm, loving woman who is dynamite in the sack. It was the first time in a while I felt safe.

As the sun crept through the curtains in my bedroom, Judy leaned over and gave me a kiss, before leaving to get ready for work. "Call me tonight," she said softly.

There was a woman in my life—I had love. I could get to work now. Forget exploring themes, the words were ready to flow. I didn't want Judy to feel obligated to represent me, but I'm sure she'd insist. I'd let the laptop power up while I brushed my teeth. After a thorough flossing, I dressed and headed back to the computer to write.

Wait. I was crazy hungry.

Eggo waffles occurred to me. Did I have any left? I checked the freezer. None. No way could I focus on an empty stomach. I'd hit Ralphs super-fast, stock up on the Eggos and syrup. I should check with Don, in case he needed anything.

The lobby chair was still outside his door.

Something was off. I knocked on the door, louder than usual. I pressed my ear against it. There wasn't a sound. Getting nervous, I pounded harder. He was so weak I had a hard time imagining he went out on his own. I'd get the key and let myself in.

Heading down the stairs, Jonas accosted me. Wearing cut off denim shorts, tank top and flip-flops, his hair was tussled and he looked hungover.

"Rupert ... Rupert ... Rupert ... Man, look at this picture I shot last night. Unbelievable." He might still be drunk.

Jonas held out his iPhone. I hoped there wouldn't be swollen male genitalia involved. Thankfully, it looked like your regular group of LGBTs: you had your bears, gay-listers, show and drag queens, art fags, a couple of twinks and a pair of bleach-blonde, bourbon-drinking 70-year-old lesbos. The regulars.

"Seems like you guys were having fun."

"Look closely." Jonas pointed to a translucent, floating ball amongst the faces.

"What is that?"

"It's her."

"Who?"

With his fingers, Jonas spread the picture to enlarge the image. "It's my fucking ghost, man. It's her."

"Holy shit!" A woman's face, crying, was clear as day.

"Yeah. After we took the picture, my friend Butch saw her face. We kept trying to talk to her, but she was unresponsive. Oh, and I'm gonna move."

"Sounds like she's harmless."

"I'm not moving because of her. My parents are buying me a loft downtown." He disco danced backwards down the hallway.

This future homeowners association would turn into a lynch mob once this chain-smoking-in-common-areas, loud-cell-phone-talking, stair-stomping club-music-playing narcissist moved in.

The Magician, Marie, now Jonas. The building was emptying out. Was I being left behind? People were moving on.

I'd stay. I was in a relationship now.

Back at Don's apartment, key in hand, I banged on his door before letting myself in. Opening the door, I noticed the curtains were drawn, it was dark, and there was a musty smell. It took me a few seconds to spot Don on the floor, flat on his back.

Please don't let him be dead.

"Rupert ... is that you?" Don could barely speak.

Kneeling beside him. "What happened?"

"You're a godsend."

"How long have you been like this?"

"Two, three days ..."

"That's horrible. What can I do?"

"Please help me up."

I tried to lift him off the floor, couldn't. He was deadweight.

"What are you doing about that oak tree blocking the driveway?" It was Brenda sticking her head in the door.

"What?"

"It came down in the storm last night."

Brenda seemed oblivious to the fact that Don was splayed out, semi-conscious on the floor. I gestured toward Don.

"What the hell's going on in here?"

"Help me get him up."

"I thought somebody had stolen that chair." She was gesturing at the one outside the door.

"Brenda ..."

"It's bad when old people fall. DON. D-I-D Y-O-U B-R-E-A-K Y-O-U-R H-I-P?"

"He's not deaf."

"Okay. Let's get you up, old man." The red pig—displaying an unexpected quickness for an obese, middle-aged woman—squatted on the floor like a sumo wrestler, lifted Don to a sitting position, wrapped her arms around his torso, deepened her squat, took a grunt, then jumped up, pulling Don with her. They both landed in a standing position. Brenda maneuvered Don with ease to the couch and sat him down. It had been impressive to watch.

Without missing a beat: "You know that fucker Hat Guy tossed my Mikey in the dumpster."

"Don. When was the last time you ate?"

"I don't know."

"I didn't even have a chance to bury him. Heartless prick."

"Don. Let me get you some water."

"You'd better get that dumb, lazy Mexican to deal with that tree."

"He's Guatemalan."

"Who cares?"

"Thanks for your help, Brenda." I hoped she'd take that as her cue to leave.

I brought Don the water and sat next to him.

"Oh, tell your friend Hat Guy I had his van towed, if he's looking for it. I don't think he'll be blocking my garage anymore."

"I need to deal with this."

"I get it." On the way out, Brenda took a slow, steady scan of the contents of the apartment—in case Don's condition deteriorated.

Don was still sipping the water. When he finished, he turned to me.

"Thank you, Rupert."

As he went to speak his next word, Don vomited up all the water, mixed with blood and bile.

"We're going to the hospital." He didn't have the energy to protest.

I rushed to put a clean shirt on him, knowing it would upset Don to be out in public looking that way. I'd take him myself, not wanting to risk an ambulance ride that might bankrupt us both.

I went down to pull out my car and saw the tree blocking the driveway. Now I'd have to call an ambulance.

"Mr. Rupert. I fix HVAC already."

It was Vasco, arms overflowing with more of Brenda's ill-gotten goods. Cortez emerged from the storage unit, with an even larger load.

"I can't get my car out. I gotta get the old man to the hospital."

"Oh...*el arbol.*"

Vasco dumped his haul into Cortez's arms. "*El necesita ayuda ...*"

"I help you. We take my truck."

I ran up to Don's, Vasco trailing after me, panting.

Vasco wiped the sweat off his face, as we each

put a shoulder under Don's arms. We half-carried him down the three flights of stairs and out the front door to Vasco's pickup truck, where we lifted him into the cab. Cortez had already pre-loaded the truck with the re-stolen stolen goods and had moved on to the tree. I could hear the chainsaw.

I slid in next to Don and steadied him against me. Vasco got in and adjusted the rearview mirror. Hanging from it was a saint card of a man in a black suit, which seemed odd attire for a saint.

Vasco proudly told me, "*Esta* Maximón. He is the patron Saint of the macho sex."

"Cool." I'd have to read up on this guy. And with that, we were off.

It was a short ride to the hospital, but surreal. Between Don spitting up blood and bile into his handkerchief, the aroma of cheap cologne and the bounce from the bad shocks, I started hearing the theme song from *Chico and the Man.* "Chico, don't be discouraged. The Man he ain't so hard to understand ... And a new day has begun ... things will be better. Oh yes they will for Chico and the Man. Yes they will for Chico and the Man." But Freddie Prinz was dead and Don was spitting up blood next to me.

"*El gato de la* red pig *esta muerta.*"

He seemed a little too matter-of-fact about it.

"It was a coyote."

"*Es possible* ..."

I was immediately suspicious. Had Mikey been silenced? Or, was it an act of revenge? Was an innocent coyote in the Glendale foothills being played for a patsy? We'd never know. Regardless, Vasco came through for Don and me. I gave him a salute as the truck pulled away from the entrance to the ER.

The ER waiting room had been the usual interminable wait. The TV was on way too loud, but it helped distract me from the carnage and germs.

It was Kamal in triage that ushered us into a small room toward the back of the ER, where Don was examined and put through a battery of tests. Kamal pulled me aside to discuss Don's essentially undocumented status. I explained to him that I was in the process of trying to get him signed up for Medicare, before this happened. He brought us help in the name of Dorothy, a social worker and master of Medicare and all social services. She made it her mission to get Don taken care of. He'd have physical therapy, free transportation, visiting nurses, the works. I'd send her some flowers.

While we waited for the doctors to figure things out, I made a commitment to get Don into good health. I'd plan a regime for the two of us. I'd been reading up about *Blue Zones*, communities of people living an average of a decade longer than the rest of us. I'd adapt a plan for Don and me. We'd start our mornings juicing, go on brisk walks—maybe not that brisk—then light afternoon calisthenics, a nap, early evening bingo to keep the mind alert, followed by pre-bedtime yoga/meditation to wind down the day. It'd be great.

But then Don stopped breathing. The nurse called "Code Blue" and I was hustled out of the examination room. I flattened against a wall as a wheeled stretcher was raced into the room, Don emerging unconscious moments later.

It was some time before I was allowed to look in on him. A nurse warned me it might be hard to see. She was right. Don was on a ventilator, a thick tube down his throat, his head propped back, a lifeless look in his eyes.

DATE	TRANSACTION DESCRIPTION	PAYMENT, FEE, WITHDRAWAL (-)	✓	DEPOSIT, CREDIT (+)	$
5.4.15	Whatchamacallit candy bar	1.50			2,769.38

18

It was court day, Friday—the culmination of an emotional week. Don had undergone surgery to remove a tumor from his intestinal tract on Tuesday. The doctors were optimistic, and Don was starting to come around. I was relieved.

The insanity of this week had been an obstacle to connecting with Judy. I was running back and forth to the hospital, dealing with doctors, Medicare, etc. But knowing she was in my life was a comfort. I'd left her a few messages and hadn't heard back. I'm sure her week was insane too.

Despite the events of the week, I was prepped for court. I'd packed a discrete, insulated soft cooler with supplies, including string cheese and baby carrots to keep my blood sugar up. My notes were thorough and comprehensive, so the whiny-voiced Jew defense lawyer or sexy silk-bloused prosecutor wouldn't get the best of me. What did worry me, was Eli. Would he stare me down while I was on the stand, eyeballing me like a crazed killer? Gesturing to his meth dealer buddies seated behind him, indicating that if my testimony favored Jonas, I'd never get out of the courthouse bathroom alive? While I had a civic duty to perform, I wasn't stupid. I'd see how strong Eli's intimidation tactics were.

I was putting the final touches on my court outfit when my phone beeped. I'd chosen a non-descript, non-threatening everyman look—an inviting light-blue polo shirt, beige Dockers and a brown, lightweight bomber jacket. I'd barely be noticed.

It was Larry.

"I have some news for you." His accent seemed thick today. He must have been excited about something.

"What?"

"We found a buyer for the building." He sounded like Goebbels.

"I didn't know it was for sale."

"We had to dump it. Between the bad plumbing and bad electrical, we'd never survive."

"How'd you sell it?"

"The Danforth Group is a crafty bunch."

"Congratulations then, I guess."

"I wanted to let you know ASAP. The new owner is planning on self-management. It'll be a quick escrow, Rupert. You'll need to figure out your situation."

"I'm out?"

"Afraid so, Rupert. The new owner will be in touch."

I thanked Larry for the opportunity.

8:15 a.m. and I was out of a job, possibly my home, and facing an awkward pat-down after going through the courthouse metal detector.

Insulated soft cooler in hand, I shored myself up and went out to face the day head-on. I ran into Hat Guy.

He was wearing a bright-orange vest with silver reflective strips, leaning into a builder's level mounted on a tripod. In his left hand he had a measuring wheel. His bowler was still in place.

"What's with the outfit?"

"Dude. Surveying MY new property."

"What are you talking about?"

"Danforth and his Aryan don't know jack about running a property like this. We haggled hard, but I finally got my deal. First thing, De Soto's gone. I'll let Danforth tell him. And then Ronnie and I will transform these grounds. We're gonna compete with the Huntington Gardens."

I was concerned for Hat Guy. "You hired someone to inspect the building, right?"

"Ef those stupid, high-priced on-the-take inspectors. Ronnie and I checked it out. He's a total pro."

"There are issues with the building."

"I'm all good, man. I'll be lord and master. Speaking of which, Rupert. Hope they're no bad feelings. Ronnie will be managing. Not that you didn't do a good job ..."

"I get it."

"No more bullshit from the tenants. And guess who's switching parking spaces with me?"

It would get ugly. "She does have the best spot."

"I hope you stay. I'll give you a good deal on rent."

"Cool." I had a lot to think about.

"Can you take three paces to the left? You're blocking the property line."

The courtroom was packed with a bunch of middle-aged white guys in cheap suits. I hadn't seen that many since my cousin Rivke's Bat Mitzvah.

I was surprised to see Judy there. I didn't even know she'd been summoned. She looked great in a floral-patterned spring look. Her hairstyle seemed softer. Had she gone to the salon this week? I had a lot to talk to her about. Fortunately, my woman was a great listener.

She didn't see me. But Jonas did. He was right across the aisle, trying to look as conservative as he could. He wore skinny black jeans, a flouncy lavender shirt and wide brocade tie, circa the 1970s. Had I underdressed?

Jonas was overtly gesturing to get my attention, pointing out Magellan and his new mini-me-boyfriend. They were leaning into each other, whispering and giggling. It was *Mean Girls*.

I was getting bored and tense waiting for Eli to emerge orange jump-suited, taking baby steps in a tangle of chains and cuffs. To calm my nerves, I felt under my seat to make sure no one had tried to steal my cooler, which anchored me. It was still there.

The bailiff called Eli's case. I immediately tensed up and snuck a string cheese from the cooler and tore off little pieces to eat, so no one could see.

Two guys looking nothing like a Jew lawyer or Angie Harmon approached the bench and conferred. The bailiff called my name. I stood up, swallowing the last bits of string cheese.

"You're dismissed."

Wait. What just happened? Which attorney feared my testimony? It was damning on both sides. In any event, I was spared a confrontation with Eli and the cheap-suited lawyers. I decided to wait for Judy on the courthouse steps.

Nearing lunch, I was gnawing on a thick carrot end when I heard the click-clack of heels behind me. Some sort of transference must have taken place between Hat Guy and me, because I instantly identified the footsteps as Judy's. I got up.

She stopped and stood next to me. "What a

waste of a morning."

"They dismiss you too?"

"I gotta get out of here. It smells." She continued walking.

I walked with her. "Great. Let's go out for a nice lunch. There's a place near here that ..."

"... I'm booked." She kept walking.

"Okay. Later, then. We have a lot to catch up on. It's been an unbelievable week."

A black Tesla S pulled up, right in front of us. A very handsome, super well-dressed, youngish, dark-skinned black man got out of the driver's side and leaned on the roof. "Yo, girl. How'd it go in there?"

"Hey, baby. Just give me a sec." She turned back to me. "I don't know what you think is going on here. We are not anything. It was an okay fuck. And I'm not interested in you or your writing."

They got in the car and drove off.

I felt sick to my stomach, wanted to throw-up. How could I let myself believe Judy was anything but the bitch I knew she was? Had my isolation at the building made me susceptible to her game?

I needed to ground myself fast. I dialed the phone and heard that weird international ringing sound.

"Is this your one phone call from jail?"

"No. Where are you?"

"Cruising the Bosphorous. You?"

"I just got shit on outside the Glendale courthouse."

"Tell me."

I told him.

The Magician explained that this was my

opportunity to exercise the Buddhist principle of turning poison into medicine. By challenging difficult situations or obstacles, we can heal ourselves. The Dryden Arms experience would serve as a catalyst for gaining a deeper form of happiness and well-being. I liked it.

"Rupert, you know what to do."

"I hope so."

"And if you fuck it all up, I'll send you a ticket and work you into the act."

I got in the car and drove. I felt better. Found myself at the best new donut shop in Hollywood. I deserved a treat, and Don better than day olds from Heavyset. They had things I'd never seen before. I picked up an assortment of Kettle-Glazed Cronuts, Blueberry Bacon Old Fashions, Boston Crèmes and last but not least, Cruffins—a Croissant-Muffin hybrid.

I wasn't sure how good these were for either of us, but sometimes you had to feed the soul.

DATE	TRANSACTION DESCRIPTION	PAYMENT, FEE, WITHDRAWAL (-)	✓	DEPOSIT, CREDIT (+)	$
5.5.15	Eggo waffles, string cheeses, baby carrots	15.93			815.44
5.7.15	Highest speed cable/Internet	19.99			795.45
5.8.15	Kettle-Glazed Cronuts, Blueberry Bacon Old Fashions, Boston Crèmes, Cruffins	18.17			777.28

19

The West Hollywood neighborhood felt revitalized. A Blue Bottle coffee had replaced the body shop. And the strip club now had valet parking. I stopped in to check on Jerry, my old apartment manager. His lot had improved, having traced the calamities wrought on him to the feng shui totem I'd left over my door. Since he'd burned and buried it at the Hollywood Forever Cemetery's Dia de la Muerta festival, he'd gotten a new boyfriend and a healthy pet parrot. He also told me he had a vacancy.

Who would have known I'd have missed the would-be actors and actresses and trannies? They were my community. There was nothing left for me at the Dryden Arms. Don needed to give up his apartment, Vasco and I didn't have a future, it would be awkward running into Judy and a deluded polymath was in control of the building.

I was moving back to West Hollywood. Returning with a profound sense of possibility. I'd land a copywriting gig at a competing hotel chain, behave myself, and get the writing on track, for real this time.

First order of business was giving Hat Guy my notice. Next would be packing up Don's place and securing his possessions in storage, until we got him sorted out.

I finally got that brunch with LoKey, Monique and the boys. The Orc and I hit the gym a few times. He gave me some good tips.

Vasco and Cortez gifted me a set of Maximón shot glasses, Maybelline gave me a warm hug and a kiss on the cheek—although I still would have preferred a blowjob—and there was radio silence from Brenda. In a weird way, I thought she'd miss me. No one else talked to her, and I'd been her buffer with Hat Guy. He'd already served her notice to clear out the storage area. She was not pleased.

And there'd been resolution to the Pluto is/isn't a planet debate. The New Horizons flyby confirmed it was a dwarf planet. I'd been resigned to this outcome for quite some time.

In any event, I wanted to do what I could for Hat Guy. I'd typed up detailed notes for him as to the inner workings of the building and all the vendors he'd need to rely on. With origami precision Hat Guy folded it into a sleek paper airplane and sent it flying down the street.

"I told you, Ronnie and I got this."

On moving day, I'd rented a U-Haul. Hired Vasco and Cortez for the move. They'd been bounced from the building too and were now working as freelance handymen and movers. It'd been hard to find a free space for the U-Haul, as Hat Guy had brought in a team of hand-chosen laborers and their various pickup trucks loaded down with sod, ground cover and an assortment of plants for his new landscape design. It was controlled chaos. Hat Guy looked satisfied.

"Dude. I'd help you load up ... but I have to supervise these guys until Ronnie gets back from Lowe's with the treated bark." He then whispered to me. "I can't take my eyes off them for a minute."

"For sure."

Team Move spent the next couple hours carrying out my possessions and Don's. Brenda watched from behind her lacy curtains. Was she more upset at my leaving, or that she hadn't gotten her mitts on Don's furniture?

Stacking the last of the boxes inside the U-Haul, Hat Guy sauntered over. He was swallowing the last of those smoked-meat sandwiches he always raved about, washing it down with an old-fashioned glass bottle of A&W root beer.

"It's a dark day. I just found out Maybelline's moving. They need more sound proofing and higher amperage. Whatever."

"It gets worse. Jonas is gonna stay."

Hat Guy's face twitched. "What happened to his loft?"

"The homeowner's association rejected him."

With that, the front door opened and Astrid strode out. I quickly nudged Hat Guy. We both watched with observant eyes as she made her way to a green Geo, got in, and drove off.

"See. Now *that* was Astrid."

"Of course it was," I agreed.

"The roommate has a blue Honda. I saw her park it last night."

"Except the blue Honda is really a green Geo that Astrid parked there last night when she came home from work."

"Dude. I know what blue looks like."

"When was the last time you had a color-blindness test?"

Vasco was trying to track the whole Astrid conversation, but couldn't latch on.

"Once I'm done with the lawn, I'll start tailing them more consistently. I'll take Astrid and Ronnie can take the roommate. Then you'll have to face the truth."

The workers had come back from their lunch break, and Hat Guy started barking orders in broken Spanish.

I went upstairs to do one more sweep of 204 and make sure nothing had been left behind. Even without a cleaning deposit in play, I'd left the place spotless. It was as though I'd never even lived there.

LoKey leaned his head in the door.

"So this is it, man?"

"It is."

I went in for the classic half-hug move, but LoKey pulled me in for a full-hug.

"Don't be a stranger."

I made my way downstairs, and found Hat Guy inhaling the aroma from a handful of bark.

"Regulation?"

"You bet."

I handed him the apartment keys.

"I'll miss you, Rupert." We shook.

I climbed into Vasco's truck, the diminutive Cortez occupying the center seat. As we pulled away, through the side mirror, I saw Brenda storm outside and hand Hat Guy a note.

DATE	TRANSACTION DESCRIPTION	PAYMENT, FEE, WITHDRAWAL (-)	✓	DEPOSIT, CREDIT (+)	$
5.11.15	Spiderman hand cloths	15.37			1,661.91
5.30.15	U-Haul, packing tape, Vasco & Cortez	441.20			1,220.71

20

Complications from his surgery had led Don on a whirlwind tour of hospitals and nursing homes the last few months. When we knew his final release date was imminent, Dorothy the social worker gave us a list of affordable senior housing to check out.

We'd struck gold: a single, only four blocks from the beach in Santa Monica. It included three meals a day, cable TV and laundry service. The ratio of women to men was definitely in Don's favor. Adele and Bernice had already found flimsy excuses to stop by Don's room with assorted baked goods and VHS copies of *Cocoon* and *Cocoon: The Return.*

Don was thriving on the attention. While that was all well and good, I still needed him to give up his aversion to having a phone. I couldn't drive to the beach every day after work to make sure he was okay. So I insisted Don learn to use the prepaid Motorola I got him. I was first on his speed dial.

I did however have my concerns. The all-inclusive rent for such a prime location seemed low. Was this a medical testing ground for one of the giant pharmaceutical companies? Where unattached, elderly people could easily vanish? Don fit the bill: he was old, had no family and a recent near-death experience. So I made my presence VERY known to the management. Making sure they knew that if anything happened to Don, I'd blow the lid off their elder medical-experimenting ring.

That might have been part of the reason the manager was willing to buy into my plan for subsidizing Don's rent. It was still too high for him. The manager lowered Don's rent, telling him it was a government program, which in reality I covered. The new copywriting gig I'd landed, with a better salary than before, allowed me to do it. Since Don wouldn't relent and sign up for SSI or veteran's benefits, I'd resorted to subterfuge.

This week's outing with Don featured a stop at *Vidiots*, dubbed "best video store in L.A." by *Los Angeles Magazine*. A bunch of twenty-to-thirty-something indie film enthusiasts staffed the place. What was it about this demographic that required them to not own a comb or clean T-shirt or have a fundamental understanding of nutrition? They were either pudgy or rail-thin, but all had pasty-white complexions, no doubt from too much inside time watching movies.

Regardless of their hygiene and complexions, they showed Don great respect. His knowledge and enthusiasm for the film noir genre and its origins in German Expressionism was a thrill for those geeks. Between the ladies at the home and the video nerds, Don was finding his community too.

Our next stop was Venice Beach, for cold-pressed juices and sunshine. We both needed to get more serious about our diets. The donut/Cronut/Cruffin habit had gotten out of hand. Especially since I started seeing Ingrid, night manager of West Hollywood's trendiest donut shop.

We sat on a bench enjoying the view, breeze and sun. It was good to be out.

"Yoga or tai chi today?"

"You decide."

"We'll do a combination." I needed to weigh the benefits of the two. See if a hybrid plan worked. For weeks I'd been building Don into the next Jack LaLanne. It was all in the service of my book on fitness for the elderly. I had an agent interested, through a connection at work.

After leaving the Santa Monica stairs, where my plan was to eventually work Don up to taking them two at a time, it was my turn to train. I needed to keep up with Don and work off all those baked goods.

I'd remembered the renowned training methods of the Chicago Bears' Walter Payton. Sweetness, as he was known, had found "The Hill." It was a nearly 45-degree incline that he powered up and down for hours. The meat and potatoes of his off-season workout routine, it defeated the NFL stars he invited to train with him.

I had my own hill—La Cienega. The grade from Santa Monica Boulevard up to Sunset was a leg-burning, heart-pumping ordeal from the dark ages. It would lead to legs of steel coil and the oxygenation of my blood to the maximum known to man.

As I was glancing up at the Hollywood Hills homes perched on stilts overhead, my phone dinged with a text.

Hat Guy: "What's the phone number for that plumber?"

Hat Guy text number two: "Dude, you there?"

DATE	TRANSACTION DESCRIPTION	PAYMENT, FEE, WITHDRAWAL (-)	✓	DEPOSIT, CREDIT (+)	$
7.11.15	Cold-pressed juices	16.03			2,922.03

AUTHOR'S BIOGRAPHY

At the tender age of seven, Johnny Allina was traumatized not only by bad parenting but by an over consumption of sweets, his father being a high-ranking executive of an esteemed candy corporation based in the Tri-State Area. He was born with the proverbial silver spoon in his mouth on Park Avenue, and raised by partially suicidal European eccentrics. Once the money was gone, the lot of them became unglued in different ways.

He dabbled in a wide array of drugs, which he parlayed into a scholarship at coveted Bennington College, where he went on to associate with more upper-class, anxiety-ridden, somewhat suicidal, vicious eccentrics.

Having navigated all aspects of bad behavior from Park Avenue, a small village in rural Vermont, a series of low- to medium-level odd jobs, an unnamed, major hotel corporate office and ultimately an apartment building in Glendale, California, he's turned the most recent example into the novel *The Dryden Arms (House of Despair, a Comedy).*

CPSIA information can be obtained
at www.ICGtesting.com
Printed in the USA
LVOW12s1605011216
515344LV00003B/720/P

9 781519 463432